Boots and Blades

C. L. Kraemer

ISBN: 978-1-62420-420-3

Credits
Cover Artist: Designs by Ms G
Editor: Christine Young

Chapter One

Rivulets of life giving fluid slid down the razor-sharp blade; the drops lazily drifting to the growing puddle on the ground, staining the mud-caked boots of the combatant. Reaching up, the warrior swiped away sweat soaked tendrils of auburn locks plastered to her forehead.

As she contemplated the past hour's massacre, foot falls thundered to the scene of destruction.

"Goddess save us! Tiamoon! You've destroyed the melon patch! What were you thinking?"

"I need to stay sharp." The gnome warrior swung the gleaming blade over her head, flinging melon juice around the field.

"Fine. You can just take your sharpened self to the shed and bring out the wheelbarrow. Gather all the melon parts and bring them to the back door. You will roll out the dough for the pies that now have to be made as a result of your thoughtlessness."

Tia groaned as she headed to the garden trough to clean off her blade and splash fresh water over her face.

"Don't complain to me. You made the decision to destroy the garden. Now you'll have to pay the price." Tia's mother turned on her heel and stomped through the damaged vegetable rows to the fence, slamming the gate as she barreled to the cottage. "That child will be the death of me, yet!"

Shoving open the entrance to the cottage, she nearly fell in her attempt to stop from tramping her sticky boots on the freshly mopped floor. She unlaced the fine leather ties, thanking the Goddess for the blessed animal who gave so willingly of itself. Boots removed and placed in the sunniest spot on the West side of the cottage, Skye entered the efficient kitchen area of her home. By the time she'd pulled the required dishware for baking, and stoked the wood stove to the appropriate temperature, Tiamoon's bedraggled form crossed the threshold heading for her room.

"Not so fast, young lady."

"But I'm sticky, and my clothes are soaked in juice."

"Not my doing. Get over here and start preparing the dough for shells to pre-cook. Maybe next time you'll think before taking out your aggressions on my garden."

"I doubt it." Tia mumbled as she dragged her stocking-clad feet toward the kitchen area.

"What?" Skye turned a steely stare her daughter's direction.

"Nothing."

"I'd best not hear grumbling from you. You've been in a right foul mood lately. What is your problem?" Skye tied the baking apron in the back and pushed up her sleeves to wrestle the melon parts into the sink for a thorough rinsing.

Tia wiped the back of a flour caked hand across her damp forehead leaving behind a white streak as wide as a skunk's stripe. "How many of these are you going to make?" Tia had assisted in the kitchen enough times to forego the formal measuring for 'pinches and dashes' of ingredients.

Skye glanced at the assorted melon parts littering the top of her counter. "Looks to be about six, but make eight shells. If we have any leftover, I'll make shepherd's pie."

Tia looked up and let her gaze wander to the window. "Mmmm. Shepherd's pie."

Skye glanced her direction and burst into laughter. A frown as thunderous as an August rain storm covered the gnome warrior's face. "What?"

Skye clutched her stomach and pointed Tia's direction.

2

"Your…your face!" She exploded into peals of laughter giving herself the hiccups in the process.

Tia rid her hands of the flour she held. She stomped into the bathroom, slamming the heavy wooden door shut. Skye feared the sound of shattering glass but was caught off guard when she heard the reverberation of laughter. The door swung open, and Tiamoon appeared with a wide grin on her face.

"I am a sight, aren't I?"

Skye could do no less than agree. The little warrior straightened her flour splotched jerkin and, with a resigned sigh, moved to the counter to continue her pie crust duties.

Skye put the last piece of cleaned melon on the drying towel. "Seriously, Tia, what is causing you such consternation? I've never seen you so unsettled."

Tia cut shortening into the flour and salt mixture. She stopped and turned to her mother. "I think, Mom, you've actually answered a question I've been asking myself. There is peace in the valley. The night elves have withdrawn to tend to their own affairs, and the rest of the folk seem quite content to let things be as they are. Yet, I feel anxious and find myself snapping at others around me. I tried, really tried, to figure out what the problem could be."

Skye listened to the pained musings of her daughter. "What was the word I said?"

"Unsettled."

"Yes, you've prowled the perimeter of our farm in the evenings setting my teeth on edge. What are you looking to find?" Skye had taken up a sharpened blade to relieve the melons of their skins.

"That's it, mother. While the rest of the valley, and most of our neighbors, is quite content to revel in this hard-won peace, I can't bring myself to slog through the days, each one as unremarkable as the last, until the end of time. I'm glad the valley rests, but I need to be moving, fighting, not sure of where the next step will take me. What am I to do?"

Skye watched the shoulders of her brave warrior daughter sag.

Her body language screamed defeat. *I'll have to find something to keep her spirits up, but what?* She lost herself in the preparations of pie meats allowing her mind to freely wander. Deep in thought, she was startled when a mouse messenger suddenly stood before her, envelope in mouth. Skye wiped her hands on her apron and gently removed the message from the creature's mouth.

"Thank you." The little grey creature sat on its haunches and waited. It was customary to offer the messenger a treat when you were no longer in need of its services.

Skye opened the envelope and pulled out the folded letter. She recognized the spindly writing of her older sister, Luna. Violently opposed to Skye's association with a night elf, she moved beyond the mountains.

They'd only visited once when Skye fled the household. The man's children were determined to provide her a living hell on earth. She grew tired of the constant bickering. Too many times pranks sworn to be harmless had come within inches of ending her life. Skye loved her night elf, but opted for love lost and life rather than death.

"What does Luna want?" she mused.

"Won't know until you read the letter, will you?" the mouse piped up.

Skye jumped having completely forgotten about the waiting messenger. "True."

Skye,

It has been many years since we corresponded. With peace in your valley, I felt confident I could write a letter, and it would be certain to arrive at your door. I need to make a strange request of you and hope you won't think me mad.

We are experiencing a wave of unusual happenstances. Our neighbors' children have been disappearing at mid-month then reappearing several moons later acting very—oddly.

So far, we've lost half a dozen youngsters. There doesn't seem to be a pattern of males or females, just children, ages five to twelve. It happened again last night. As you can imagine, the families are quite distraught and confused.

Would you be able to send Tiamoon over? My next-door neighbor, Killian, has been trying to follow up, but there are more disappearances than he can handle. He could use some assistance.

I received reports of her prowess with a blade, and hope she will be able to work with him to solve this riddle.

Please send an answer with the messenger—either way.

Your sister,

Luna

Skye scribbled a response and handed the messenger the scrap of paper. She noted the creature eyeing one of the pies. Wrapping the pastry in waxed paper and securing it with rubber bands, she placed the tart inside the bag on its back.

"I hope that will suffice as payment."

"I believe so. Thank you." The mouse messenger disappeared out the door.

Skye was wiping her hands on the apron when Tiamoon returned to the kitchen. "I believe I might have a solution to your growing restlessness."

Tia located a very small tart and took a healthy bite from it marveling at the smooth consistency of the filling. "What would that be?"

"Tia...don't talk with your mouth full."

Tia rolled her eyes. Once she cleared the food from her mouth, she repeated her question. "What would that be, mother?"

"Your aunt Luna and her village need the assistance of a skilled warrior." Skye watched her daughter sit straighter and lean toward her as she spoke.

"Go on."

"There are troubles involving the disappearance of children.

5

When the young ones return, they're different."

"How?"

"I don't have all the details. You'll have to get those from your aunt when you arrive. There could be a great deal of danger—or none at all. Sitting here at the edge of the valley won't give you answers."

Skye watched her daughter roll over the situation in her mind. If she were truly as bored as she claimed, she'd be jumping up and packing her things. This hesitation was odd.

"What's stopping you?"

"The high plains are home to many battle-tested warriors. Why me?"

Skye stared at her daughter. Was it not but this morn, she all but destroyed a year's worth of work done in the garden because she was *bored*? "Fine. I'll fetch a sparrow to bring a mouse messenger and send a note to your Aunt letting them know you won't be available to help."

Tia stared at her mother. *Why is she pushing so hard?*

Skye pulled a chair to her and plunked down. "You have wandered aimlessly around the house, ridden your horse for days on end, coming back to sit in the garden and sharpen your blade so many times, I'm amazed there is any steel left. You need a purpose, daughter. If you don't find a direction soon, I'm afraid I'll lose patience and possibly my mind.

"I love you, Tia, but domesticity is not a suit I see you wearing. Find your way."

She moved to the stove to fix a cup of tea. When she'd applied the proper amount of milk and sugar, Skye removed her apron and meandered to the living room to settle in her favorite chair in front of the fire. Pangs of guilt stabbed through her. She loved her children, but the time had come for her daughter to strike out on her own.

Wood crackled in the fireplace, and the familiar sound coupled with the warmth of the flames soothed Skye's angst. She would always welcome her offspring to visit, but it was time for her to begin to live. There were places beyond the valley she wanted to visit. She continued to ruminate about her situation when she felt the warmth of a hand on her shoulder.

"I'm sorry, mom. I had no intention of causing you such grief. I'm a warrior without a war. A long trip to the other side of the mountains might be just what I need to work out where I'll put my energies when I return."

Skye felt her neck muscles tense.

"I'm sure there are several places where I can hang my hauberk until I settle."

Skye resisted the urge to let her guilt push her into making a rash statement. "Daughter, you are welcome to stay here for a couple weeks. However, I believe it is time you struck out on your own. Whether you do or don't pair does not matter. Living in your own place is a freedom you need to experience."

Tia chuckled. "Don't worry, mom. I won't come back and haunt you." Tia snatched up her bags and pushed through the back door to the small barn out back. Every journey began with a single step.

Chapter Two

High Desert, Central Oregon

Killian stared at the rise of rock from the desert floor. The emerging sun tricked the sky into revealing pink and blue streamers across the horizon exposing the severe lines of craggy mountains. Pine trees scented the air, and the slightest hint of sage tickled his nose.

"Where are they disappearing to? They're much too young to be running away."

"Master Killian?"

The young man turned his blue gray eyes from the mountain to answer. "Yes, Ms. Luna. What can I do for you?"

"Are you sitting out here at this early hour worrying about the young ones?" Luna's black hair was braided down her back and she sported a shawl bright with her clan's colors. She handed the young man a steaming cup of coffee. "I hope you don't mind black. I've yet to milk the goat."

Killian flashed her a seldom seen smile. "Ms. Luna, you make the best coffee in the desert. Black is fine."

Taking up a spot next to him on the porch, she turned her attention to the mountains admiring the soft colors of rose and tan springing to life in the morning sun. "What is it that haunts you so?"

"The illogicality of it all."

"Aye, I figured that. It is indeed illogical. The children are too responsible to leave unannounced, yet they are snatched from their beds in the middle of the night with no clues."

Killian sipped the wicked black brew and allowed the liquid to spike his taste buds. The brilliant light of a new day was caressing the landscape and warming the air. "The kinders disappearing are not inclined to run off. They are the eldest and mo st reliable. These missings make no sense. They don't happen in the same area or at the same time. They're completely arbitrary and being so—random—has given me pause to find a method. If I were to discover a pattern, the recovery would be simpler."

Luna watched the anguish distort his handsome young face. His blue eyes clouded to a dark grey when he spoke of the missing children, and his normally full mouth stretched to a tight slash across his face.

"I don't wish to sound cruel, but none of these are young ones of your own family. Why take their absence to heart?"

Killian relaxed his scowl a bit, and a smile began to touch his lips. "Because it is they who will be the leaders of our clans in but a few short years. I had hoped to retire my sword someday to warm my boots by a fire. Having a mate and young ones around isn't such a bad idea."

He automatically sipped his dark brew. *It would indeed be nice to warm my feet by a fire with a mate and children. The problem being I've found no person who makes me think in such terms.*

"Well, I must admit, Master Killian, I never would have thought you to be the settling type." She picked up his cup, returning from the kitchen minutes later with fresh coffee in the container.

"Neither had I, Ms. Luna, neither had I, howe ver, aside from our missing young ones, there has been no conflict between the clans, nor have the Others tried to interfere in our affairs in a very long time. It is a good thing for many but for me, what good is a warrior without a war?"

Luna could only agree with his forlorn assessment; what good, indeed, was a warrior without a war? "Maybe a solution will arrive in the near future. You never know."

Killian shrugged his shoulders. Who knew indeed?

Chapter Three

Outside Eugene

Tia checked the saddlebags one more time and tugged on the cinch of the saddle now affixed to Pony.

"I'll do as much walking as I can, but there will be times I'll need to use your assistance."

Pony humphed. "If you must. I'd much rather stay here and graze in the field. It looks as though it's going to be a beautiful spring, and I'd like to enjoy it quietly."

"Yes, wouldn't we all? If you complete your part of the journey with little complaining, I'll retire you from service. Will that be enough of an incentive?"

Pony turned to eye Tia. "Is that a promise?"

She dipped her head in acknowledgment.

"You swear on your sword you will turn me out to the field and never use me again as a warrior horse?"

"On my sword."

"Then let's get this journey underway." Pony impatiently tramped her feet.

Tia laughed. It surprised her that getting Pony's assistance was so easily won. She grabbed the pommel and swung into the saddle, settling in for a long ride. As she lifted the reins and readied to set off, her mother came trotting toward her from the house.

"Tia! Tia!" She slowed to a walk and stopped to catch her breath. Shoving a wrapped box at her daughter, she said, "This is for your Aunt Luna. I will trust you to honor my wishes and not open the package.

Your word?"

Tia huffed an exasperated breath. "Why is it today everyone wants me to give my word? Yes, mother, I will make sure the package gets to Aunt Luna unopened. Can you please place it in the saddle bag?"

Skye unlatched the leather bag and slipped the box on the top. "Thank you. Safe journey, daughter."

"Thank you, Mother. I will send message via the mouse network when I arrive."

"I'll wait for word of your arrival." Skye watched as Tia and Pony set a brisk pace toward the eastern horizon. "Goddess, please watch over her. She is a rash, yet brave, warrior. I may not wish her to live in my house, but I do wish her to be in my life for a while longer." With her quick prayer uttered, Skye returned to her home.

~ * ~

Tia and Pony made substantial progress their first day. When the sun cast its last light, they had secured a clearing by the river near a small area designated Vida. Tia could be seen by the Others and Pony was visible too because she was, well, a pony. However, Tiamoon learned early in her life that Others were prone to either dismiss or antagonize those they didn't understand. Keeping out of their way eliminated problems.

She ruminated on her history. The product of a bizarre pairing of gnome and night elf, Tiamoon walked her own path. Her mother's happiness had been viciously cut short by her stepchildren. Tia kept the verbal and, oft times, physical torment she'd experienced to herself. She could see how her mother struggled to make the hardest decision any person can make—stay in an impossible situation because of love of a man, or leave and live in peace with the child you love more than life itself.

"I can only hope I never have to make the same choice." Tia shifted her weight and punched the bunched-up blanket folded against

Pony's saddle. Quickly settling for the night, the gnome warrior was soon sleeping. Pony curled her body against her companion and drifted into dreamless slumber.

For two days, Tia and Pony rode then camped, dropping into deep sleep once the fire had been extinguished. By the third day of their journey, they sensed the gradual increase of elevation. Evergreens were more abundant. What little sign of human civilization could occasionally be glimpsed in the prior days disappeared. There was naught but nature to accompany the pair.

"Finally. Blissful quiet." Tia pulled deeply of the mountain air.

"We are not alone." Pony shook her mane as she flicked her ears. "I hear faint scrabbling in the bush."

"Stop and we'll just listen." The pair halted amid a copse of spruce, Tia dismounting and strained their auditory abilities.

"Maybe I was..." Pony started.

"Shh!" Tia squinted her eyes creating a crease in her forehead. Pony's ears were attuned to the sounds of outside. If she said she heard a noise, one could bet there was something lurking in the brush. The woods were uncharacteristically quiet; nothing was making noise.

"I believe we do have an observer."

"Where..." Pony started to jerk her head around to peruse the area.

"Stop!"

Pony tensed her muscles. "If there is a predator about, I wish to know where—to be able to defend myself."

Tia clenched her teeth together as she spoke lowly. "I understand, but the more noise we make guarantees our stalker will fade into the shadows giving him the advantage over us."

"Mmm. Right."

Pony proceeded to take a solid stance, breathing so shallowly Tia was afraid she would pass out. The silence unnerved the pair, and they opted to venture further on the path through the thick woods; Tia in front, Pony's lead clutched tightly in her hand. Air clung heavily to their bodies. Carefully placed footfalls resulted in leaf crunching sounds on the forest floor. Light lessening with each step belied the fact it was near the noontime meal.

Tia turned to Pony. "The woods hide their secrets from us. I sense movement and feel the presence of gazes upon us, but can't determine the source. Instincts are urging me to run, but I don't want to give in to unfounded fear."

Pony snorted. "I don't care who knows I'm afraid. Jump on my back, and let's move quickly through this quagmire of death."

Tia tended to agree with Pony's assessment and swung up to the saddle. They moved at a clipped pace focusing on a bright spot on the horizon. When they emerged into the brightness of the day, both breathed a heavy sigh of relief.

"I can safely say I've never experienced anything like that in my entire life." Tia settled comfortably in the saddle.

"Nor have I." Pony slowed to a trot. "And I think I can say I don't wish to do it again."

Tiamoon patted Pony's neck. "Me neither."

Trudging a bit further, they realized the path was slowly slanting toward the rising mountains. They were leaving the even cushion of the forest floor and entering rock strewn, narrow trails traversed by few but the mountain goats. After a brief time of climbing, Tia pressed her legs against Pony's sides.

"What?"

"I'm going to dismount and walk from here. The pathway we're on won't be getting easier, and I feel there is no sense in you straining any more than me."

Pony pulled to a stop. "Thank you."

Tia slid from her perch and gingerly set her boots on the uneven ground. She stood still and listened. A few birds whistled and flit through the sky. All seemed well, but Tia felt unsettled; her skin itched and the hair on the back of her neck prickled. She glanced at Pony and noted the hair of her mane near her neck stiffened.

"You feel it too?"

"Yes."

The skitter of pebbles echoing from a location nearby set the two reconnoitering the surrounding area. Moving up the trail, the pair crested a ridge to view a beautiful meadow, tall grasses waving in the cool spring breeze. A small lake reflected the blue sky dotted with cotton candy white clouds scurrying to the north.

Tia turned to Pony. "Suddenly, I'm very tired. What say we find a spot and settle in for the rest of the day and night?"

Pony shook her mane. "Sounds heavenly; let's go."

The rocky walkway graduated to a spongy meadow grass soothing the aching appendages of the pair. A small grove of trees hugged the shore of the body of water. Tia headed the direction of the protected site, Pony lagging behind. She waited and unloaded the small horse dropping the items on the cushioned surface. With a practiced hand, she freed her friend from all her encumbrances and scratched her back.

"Oh, that feels so good. Would you rub my face? It's been so long since you put on my halter, my jowls feel chapped."

Tia obliged and felt the horse sag in relief. Once the ritual was completed, Pony wandered off to graze, and the warrior gnome searched for firewood to start her dinner. When she collected enough downed limbs, she piled them in an area protected by the boughs of the trees, ensuring the limbs would stay usable for the fire. The glow of the flame and bit of warmth provided settled over the pair, comfortably supplying a minimal sense of security. Tia pulled the saddlebags to her position and rummaged through the contents to find the packages her mother tucked in the bottom. A small kettle sealed with a wax cover and wrapped in several layers of kitchen clothes rested against the leather container. Next to it was a paper wrapped item emitting a saliva producing smell. Tia pulled the fresh baked bread and kettle from the bag. Carefully bending the wax from the kettle, she set the container on the rock platform she erected over the embers. A peek into the pot insured her the stew was her mother's best and would fill her stomach with warmth and nutrition.

Skye, Tia's mother, was as gifted a cook as she was a healer. Tonight's dinner proved the known fact. Once Tia had eaten until she hungered no longer, she allowed the kettle to cool and, with great skill, attached the wax cover to ensure none of the life-giving liquid would escape. As she slid the container back into the saddlebag, her hand scraped against another metal form. She grasped the round pan and pulled it to her. Carrying the treasure to the campfire, Tia let her hopes soar. Her mouth watered in anticipation, but she knew impatience wouldn't serve her well.

"Pony?"

"Hmm?"

"Is there anything else I can do for you?"

A moment of silence passed. "No, I believe I'm fine now. Let me sleep, and I'll be happy."

Tia had to smile. Pony loved her sleep, almost more than grazing.

"Sleep well, my friend." She sat on a log she'd drawn up near the rock ringed fire and, with utensils in hand, untied the string around the second pot. Before her eyes was her favorite sweet pie—blackberry cobbler. Even cold, Skye's cobblers would temp the angels from the heavens. Sweet tooth sated and her utensils and crockery cleaned, the warrior gazed into the flickering of flames wishing she had the ability to see the future in the manner of the soothsayer at home. The heat radiated from the logs, pushing away the cool evening air and seducing Tia's eyelids to flutter. She struggled to stay awake. *Wouldn't do to get our throats cut tonight.* Standing, she recognized she would need to step away from the inviting heat and keep her eyes open. *I'll sleep when we've finished our task.*

~ * ~

The smell meandering through the wood on the gentle breeze was familiar, a recognizable aroma from a previous time long ago. He was confused as to why his mouth watered. His inclinations had changed in the last few months. Enda crept nearer the glowing embers. A container with a lid captured his attention as the source of the hunger producing vapors. He moved toward the pot, but halted when he sensed movement near the fire. A being was sitting on a log facing the banked fire, back to him.

He sniffed the air. It was female as was the pony snoozing near the forest line. Few travelers ventured into these woods. The Others forged through the mountains to the desert in the East by hacking out a travel way and putting a hard rock surface on the path. They were so busy whisking past in their motorized carriages, they ignored activities happening right next to the road. Few willingly choose to venture through the wilderness.

Enda's curiosity increased. He tiptoed near the figure. Moving with practiced stealth, he stood staring at the back of the female. The she-creature lifted her head and released a sigh. He sensed her surfacing from a deep pool of concentration. Head tilting to catch sounds, her hand moved to the shining weapon at her side. The she creature sprang up from the log seat and turned to face him, a look of confusion crossing her face, then a flash of terror as she snapped the weapon into a ready position.

"AAAHHHHH!"

The war cry assaulted his ears. Wings flipping out, he bared his teeth, eyes flashing red. The curiosity that drove him to seek out this being was replaced by the will to survive. Enda launched into the air, catching a wind current. His keening echoed through the trees.

Chapter Four

West Foothills, Cascade Mountains

Ants. Millions of ants crawling on her body. Tiamoon's ears focused on the noise of movement behind her. Bursting into her fighting stance, she ripped the silence with a war whoop while swinging her blade to the ready, finding herself standing face-to-face with a...gnome? A face somewhat familiar to her. The eyes were tinged deep red, whites appearing bloodshot and upper teeth extending over the bottom lip. Panic oozed from the creature as it snapped out a set of leathery wings and bolted into the sky, releasing an ear-splitting keening and disappearing into the night sky.

Recognition slowly crept into Tia's memory. "Enda," she whispered. One of the bravest warriors she'd fought alongside during the early clashes in the old country.

"What the hell happened?"

Fully aware now, she paced back and forth in front of the dying embers. When the rush of adrenalin subsided, Tia placed another log on the fire pit and gazed into the dancing flames. Her pensive mood led her to deeply buried memories; days spent hunkered down in dark, dank caverns sharing whispered battle strategies.

Enda led her group through deadly clashes and weeks of dodging the enemy. He'd mended bones with his limited magic skills and bolstered flagging morale with passionate discussions about the beauty of home and warmth of hearth. He'd suffered losses none of the warriors knew save Tiamoon.

A rival clan leader had kidnapped his only sister. An extensive search of the surrounding hills and dales produced nothing. His abrupt halt to the quest surprised all except her aunt, Luna, and she did not speak to the reason. Yet, he picked up his courage and led others to fight for their villages and clans.

Seeing him in such an unnatural state upset her more than she could express. The reason for her journey to her aunt's had been something of a mystery. She now felt honor bound to find Enda and determine the reason for his—change. *This will give me a purpose to continue.*

The sky's ominous darkness lessened, stars dimming with the onset of the new day. A ribbon of pale pink crushed against the mountain peaks. Pony stirred and set to grazing on the sweet meadow grass.

"Don't gorge yourself," Tia warned. "We've a long way yet to go."

"Yes, and I'll need energy to make the trek successfully."

"Well spoken. Allow me to indulge in a warm cup of coffee before we clean up the area and depart." She pulled a small metal container from the saddlebags and strolled to the clear lake. Dipping the pan in the cold reservoir of mountain water, she found herself staring eye-to-eye with a multi-colored fish.

"Morning," she acknowledged as she leaned on her heels. "How is the day treating you?"

The silver creature fanned its tail lazily. *I can only speak for myself, but so far, I am pleased with the results. And you?*

Tia allowed a grin to lighten her face. "I believe I can concur with your assessment."

The fish turned and meandered away from the shore. Tia started to feel miffed until she realized there was nothing more to say. While the mountain creature was quite loquacious by most standards, the processing of its thinking was simple—no need to hang around and risk capture after the niceties had been exchanged.

Straightening from her crouched position, she pulled of the fresh morning air. A few well-placed strides and she was at the banked fire.

A few small branches added to the waning flames after rearranging the cooled rocks in the center, and Tia placed the pan with crystal clear water in the center to heat for coffee. It wasn't long before the water roiled and popped sending sizzling drops to the rocks beneath. She pulled fresh ground beans from her personal pouch and gently sprinkled them in the water. Within the blink of an eye, the aroma of coffee permeated the clearing. Tia poured the liquid from the pot into her cup and, taking a sip, savored the robust flavor.

When she finished her drink, she cleaned her cup while securing the food containers. Several pans of water later, the fire pit had been transformed to a mud pit ensuring there would be no danger of setting the woods aflame.

"Sorry, Pony, but we must continue with our eastward journey."

A wistful sigh escaped the lips of the small horse as she moved to allow Tia to saddle her and place their supplies on her back. A twinge of longing tugged at rider and pony as the wisp of a breeze caressed their backs.

"We must remember this location for our journey home," Tia squinted against the rising sun, thankful of a slender band of clouds drifting across the bright orb. They'd plodded for an hour noting the rise of the road and increase of jagged rocks jutting from the path. Again, the skittering of pebbles disturbed the sounds, or lack thereof, above the trekking pair. Tia's skin prickled and Pony's mane hair bristled.

"We are being tracked," Pony noted. Tia grunted her agreement. They increased the speed by which they moved over the animal trail frequently checking their surroundings. It soon became evident the stop in the meadow would increase their travel time through the rough mountain terrain.

"As much as I hate to think of it, we need to be careful of our footfalls. I would rather lose time than my life." With grudging agreement, Pony slowed her pace and picked up her hooves with more prudence. The trail sloped upward at a forty-five degree angle giving the intrepid travelers cause to stop and catch their breath halfway up the incline.

Deep rumbling and waterfalls of pebbles startled the pair. The earth beneath their feet shook throwing them off balance creating the need to grapple for a place to grab. Screeching of granite against granite sucked the silence from the air and a huge boulder crashed behind them cutting off their passage to the west. Once the cascade of rock s and dirt subsided, the pair turned panic-stricken faces to each other.

"We're stuck," Pony huffed through her nose.

"So we are. Let's travel until the sun reaches the zenith of the sky, and we'll locate a place to rest and eat for the night. I believe ou r bravery and courage will be tested."

From a distance, many eyes tracked the movement of the pair.

Chapter Five

High Desert, Central Oregon

He woke with a start. All night he'd tossed and turned seeing the faces of the missing children in his troubled mind. Rising from his sleep pallet, Killian dragged his hand across sleep filled eyes. A container of water stood on a small chest of drawers for his use.

The shock of cold against his face sucked the air from his lungs and chased any further thoughts of rest into the light of day. Taking the fresh cloth from the side of the bowl, Killian quickly cleansed his person before donning his outerwear.

Bread, water and fresh vegetables were laid neatly on his kitchen counter, where he straddled a long-legged stool and consumed his meal. Unsure of what he could do differently, Killian knew sitting around waiting for a solution to present itself wasn't the answer. It behooved him to be in the mountains searching. The children weren't going to be found in the villages. The longer he waited, the less likely the chances were he'd pick up a trail. Shoving the remaining bread and vegetables in a knapsack, he placed the bag at the front entry. He tugged on his boots, grabbing the coat he lay next to the door last evening before retiring for the night, and was slipping into it when he heard a rap upon his door.

He opened to find Luna holding a knapsack.

"If I have deduced correctly, Master Killian, you are on your way to the mountains." The chagrined expression on his face gave her the answer she knew to be correct. "I'm sure you have some supplies to take with you, but I've brought fresh baked bread and a small portion of a sweet cake for those trying times when you need a lift."

"I know...we know...you are doing the best you can, but don't expose yourself to excessive danger."

Killian ushered her into his abode offering her a seat. "I cannot, in good faith, consider my own safety above that of the children."

Luna graced him with a tender smile. "That is not what I spoke. My wish is for you to take care of yourself and come home unharmed. I feel certain you will rescue our young ones."

"Sitting about and trying to deduce a plan vexes me. At least in the mountains, I'm able to count on my skills to set me on the right path. From there, it is simply skill and, unfortunately, luck."

Luna was forced to agree. "Maybe there is a way to enhance your luck. Let me search my tomes for wisdom from the ancients. I'm sure they encountered such troubles in their times."

Killian hid a smirk. Lady Luna was spell-keeper and dream weaver of the village. He had benefited from her medical expertise on more than one occasion, but he wasn't inclined to give credence to her spell weaving.

"Thank you. I don't wish to appear rude, but time is of the essence. I must utilize the light of day to my best advantage."

Luna rose from her perch. "Of course, young master. I'll keep a positive thought for your success in this matter. May your journey be full of good fortune."

He waved at the shaman as she plodded down the path to her abode. His sense of urgency was heightened by the short delay. It would be advantageous to run while the morning was cool. Once the sun neared the top of the sky, temperatures would attempt to meet the fiery ball. In a manner practiced over decades, Killian tethered his kit. Quickly securing his home, he was on the road heading toward the Cascades. He took comfort in the heft of his sword strapped across his back. The one theatre where he held no doubt was his blade abilities. He could honestly claim excellence over any in the land after dueling, and defeating, many night elf opponents.

The mountains loomed ahead, setting his heart to pounding, and quickening his pace. The pounding of his boots against the ground matched the rhythm of his heartbeat. Birds exploded into the air complaining loudly at the interruption of their peace. His concentration was so intense, he neglected to listen to his body and was perplexed when stars appeared before his eyes. Stopping to ponder the reason why, he quickly deduced he was thirsty, and his body needed a break from the arduous pace.

Looming ahead was an outcropping of boulders offering respite from the dust and sun. He slowed and, choosing a granite surface in the shade lower to the earth than the rest, relieved the pressure from his feet. The need to back off the frantic stride was necessary if he was to be of any value searching. He wriggled out of his backpack and searched inside, the crinkle of waxed paper alerting him to a small cache of sweet treasures.

Known to be quite the baker, Lady Luna had taken the time to fix Killian's favorite—small bite-sized rum cakes. His mouth watered at the thought. As he dared to hope, the first whiff of rum-soaked cake filtered past his nose. He gazed lovingly at the golden concoction before devouring the treat with the enthusiasm of a child. Licking his fingers with relish, Killian sighed contentedly.

"Thank you, Lady Luna, for the needed boost." He took time to erase his presence from the scene. The animals might sniff out his brief respite, but he wanted his stop to go unnoticed by any other passing this way. He hunted a cunning opponent; one who could steal into the homes of sleeping families and abscond with their most precious possessions — their children.

He would have to outwit his opponent.

Trudging up the quickly rising path, Killian rolled his head to rid his muscles of the stiffening starting to set in. He slowed his pace. There was—something else—nearby. His taunt neck muscles, and the rising of hair on his arms alerted him. He attempted to walk as he would were he tracking a rabbit for dinner. That's when it started; tiny rivulets of dirt showering him as he walked past the rock wall. He stopped and gazed up as far as he could see, but spotted naught but more granite. He stood in place, not moving, barely breathing. *Nothing.* As he began to move, the dirt showers started again. Killian spotted an overhang on the trail and sprinted to stand in the safety of the niche. *It is probably just a deer grazing, and it's gotten too close to the drop off. I can hope...*

Chapter Six

High in the Cascade Mountains

Patrick and Maeve squat on the edge of the boulder.

"Do you think they noticed?" Maeve wore a frown on her young face. "I want to go home to mama."

Patrick pulled the little girl from the ledge. "They may not figure out right away what was happening, but I know Master Killian will put the clues together."

The crack of a whip just above the children's heads put a halt to further conversation.

"Just where did you think you would be going, now?" A creature of unknown age towered over the pair. "You weren't thinkin' of leavin' us, were ya? We'd miss your bright and shiny faces." He snarled at the youngsters and snapped the whip just above their heads once more.

"Get your little arses up here." He jerked the chains linking the wrist irons together causing Maeve to fall and bash her knee on the rocky surface.

The little gnome cried out but bit her lip, drawing blood. A tiny trickle escaped the corner of her mouth and slowly dribbled to her chin.

Arvin, the overseer, stopped, staring at the rivulet of red fluid. His tongue snaked from his mouth and moved around his mouth, saliva glistening in the low light of the approaching eve.

Patrick noticed the overseer's large canines increasing in length. The big animal's arms hung slack at his side, his eyes quickly glazing over. He began weaving forward and backward, keening slowly, catching Patrick off-guard when he shuffled toward Maeve. Patrick yanked his chain from the overseer's hands. He snatched Maeve into his arms and barreled up the path, slipping behind an outcropping of rocks to take advantage of the momentary shelter.

Maeve snuffled. "My knee and mouth hurt."

"If we don't clean you up, Arvin will drain every drop of blood in your body. Your knee and face won't be the only thing to hurt." Grabbing any available greenery they could find, the pair wiped the blood from Maeve then scurried to catch up with the troop of other kidnapped children. Patrick nervously glanced over his shoulder, praying the overseer wouldn't snap out of his blood induced trance until they'd traveled up the path. Explanations would fall to him for his tardiness.

The band of tiny prisoners and their captors trudged toward the peak of the mountain. Three-quarters the way up in a craggy crevasse, a niche, easily hidden under a slate overhang, opened to a hidden community known to very few.

The crew leader pulled the connecting chain to snap the prisoners from their self-imposed stupors. They were housed in cells by pairs per the location from whence they were snatched. Patrick and Maeve, while not related, were from the village of the shaman Luna. Four years apart, they had merely nodded at each other in the town square prior to their abduction. A month of forced togetherness brought the two close; each depending on the other for strength. As the leader pushed Maeve through the cell door, Patrick bared his teeth and roared his fiercest when she yelped in pain.

The taskmaster, startled by the sudden aggression exhibited from the young man, stumbled, landing on his derriere. He exploded from the ground toward the dark-haired gnome with flashing green eyes. "I'll have you for myself!"

Patrick slipped past the larger creature and scooped up Maeve. "You will not harm my companion."

His dangerous tone caused the leader to hesitate—slightly. He pushed forward to the cell door, fully intent on causing the small male gnome serious physical harm.

"Stop."

The effect of the one word on the leader was stunning. Patrick gathered Maeve in his arms and backed up until he stood against the wall of the cave.

"But, sire..."

"You will cause no more harm to these children."

The taskmaster snarled at the pair bunched against the back of the cell. "You escaped—this time." He turned and stomped away.

Patrick stepped forward. "Thank you, Master Enda."

The elder gnome waved off the gratitude. "Do not aggravate the crew chiefs. I interceded this time, but I won't always be around to stop him."

"Of course, sire." Patrick watched the ginger-haired gnome stride from the cell. His demeanor spoke to that of a warrior; straight back, precision of step and keen observatory skills. *He seems so wrong for this place.*

Little did the young man know how true was his statement.

Chapter Seven

Cascade Mountains

Enda Orr peered from the edge of the cavern toward the desert floor spread below. His clan, what was left, were settled out there. Most of those he knew would be sporting glints of silver in their hair. He pushed a breath through parched lips. It was time for him to rest before his nightly hunt. This curse vexed him to no end.

*

Ireland, County Down, late 1800s

His plan had been to rescue his sister, Orla. When she demurred the proposal of marriage from the clan Chieftain, Sean McLaughlin, made at the annual summer games in the old country, none of them could imagine the plague they were setting upon the village. Sean did not appear upset by the refusal. In fact, he was quite hospitable to all of Enda's kin, inviting them to visit his clan's home in the Mourne Mountains.

The Orr clan rode south, their superior hunting skills the talk of the games.

Orla's quiet refusal of Clan Chief McLaughlin's proposal generated shocked whispers through the gnome community. She sequestered herself in the hut, seldom seeing the blue of the Irish summer sky. One fair morn, she ventured forth to pick the last of the berries to incorporate into pies and never arrived home. Enda searched every valley and glen he knew where she gathered berries. It was unlike his sister to stray too far from the village.

A week passed with no word, no sign of his sister. As he decided the time to mount a search using all the resources at his disposal had come, a messenger mouse arrived at the doorstep.

"A message for the Clan Chief Orr." It held the paper in its paw, wrapped in cloth, while sitting on its haunches.

Enda accepted the folded note. Fear clutched at his insides. A mouse message was seldom good news. Opening the paper, he found four words printed:

She is mine—forever. Sean

"Please wait." He entered the house and prepared a small bag of grain, which he carried to the waiting messenger and placed it about his neck. "No reply." The small rodent squeaked a thank you and departed. Enda stood holding the message in his hand. He was certain the blood in his veins had frozen solid. How could this have happened? When they left the clan games, all appeared well. He realized he would need to consult the shaman before attempting anything further.

~ * ~

Luna felt the presence before spying the furry messenger scurrying to Enda's home. The creature was free of aura. The note, however, vibrated black energy. It was a certainty the news Enda was about to receive was not positive. She would wait one full day before approaching the Clan leader.

She prepared a brew that needed to sit overnight to enhance the scrying potency she would call into use. The final ingredient would depend on the message contained in the note. Luna sent a quick prayer to the Earth Goddess to protect Enda and his sister, Orla, who had not been seen in seven days. The lass was but a wee wisp of gnomehood, catching the eye of many a young suitor. The gossip in the village was she'd turned down a proposal by Sean McLaughlin.

Luna shivered. He was a wicked piece of work. The foxes of the far north carried tales of witnessing blood sacrifices. Some included the tidbit that bloodletting was being done on gnomekind. Luna found this information truly disturbing, and chose not to believe it. The old magic could be easily perverted. The consequences to the practitioner were dire, one could almost say, deadly. She was so mired in ruminations, she failed to hear the footfalls approach her door.

"Luna?" Trepidation filled the voice, emphasized by the light knock.

Starting out of her reverie, she answered. "Please enter, Enda. You are welcome."

The door creaked on the hinges as the clan chief steeped through.

"Darn, I need to grease those things again."

Enda chuckled. The metal clasps provided the shaman the ability to hang a heavier wooden door, but at a price. Unless she wished to deal with a sound resembling the cry of a banshee, she was forced into manual maintenance.

Her preference would have been to magic it quiet, but such a waste of natural gifts would insult the Goddess. "What brings you to my home?" Prior knowledge did not preclude manners.

"This." He shoved the mouse message toward her.

Luna grabbed the edges of her shawl and used them to pick up the poisonous letter.

Enda eyed her actions with suspicion. "Why did you do that?"

"You are protected from most harm by a spell Orla asked me to create."

One eyebrow rose.

"She asked me in confidence because she knew of your—nonbelief—in such things. Were I to touch this item without some barrier between my skin and it, I would suffer blistered skin, which would not heal for a fortnight. Makes eating difficult."

Enda wore an expression of disbelief, but with less intensity. "Please, Luna, tell me what abomination this is." He nodded to the note.

She rummaged in her pockets for a handkerchief to use then, fingers covered by the cotton, opened the folded sheet, sucking in a deep breath. It was as she feared...worse. Enda's sister was lost to him for all eternity. The clan McLaughlin were not known for their ability to accept rejection. She moved to the banked embers in the front room fireplace and tossed in the paper. Within seconds, the sheet burst into angry blue flames shooting high into the chimney.

"Guess there'll be no need to call the sweep this year." She turned to face an angry Enda.

"That was mine!"

"Aye, and if you would have kept it to ruminate over, you would have fallen prey to the evil emanating from the spell cast over the words. Your temperament would sour, and none around you would be able to shake you from its influence. Better this way. You got the message." Her look dared him to argue with her.

The set of his jaw let her know he was still angry, but he nodded agreement. Luna took a seat and, with a motion of her hand, offered him a chair. Enda complied. She placed her hands in her lap and began to recite.

The clan has fallen into an aberration of evil so deep, there is no salvation for them. The actual event happened long ago; the date has slipped my memory. The original clan chieftain fathered a girl child so beautiful, the angels desired her. At that time, the clan resided within the Carpathian Mountains in Romania, as it is called now.

While we are small in stature, you are aware some of our people have made enormous contributions to the world of man. Even though the chieftain's daughter was taller than most of us, she was considered tiny by the human standards.

Yet, many of the village farmers as well as creatures of the crevasses lusted for her. One particular farmer, a man called Liam, was determined to make her his property. She would have nothing to do with him. He met the village healer to secure a love potion, but the shaman would not help him, stating the female of his attention was cursed and would bring nothing but sorrow to his household.

The farmer was determined, nonetheless, and offered the clan chieftain supplies from his land for a lifetime. Still, the clan leader turned down his generous offer causing the farmer great distress. Storming from the caves the gnomes called home, he stumbled about in the increasing dark.

By the time his eyes adjusted to the night light, he stood in the center of a cave whose walls were drenched in blood. His skin prickled with the idea of where all the liquid on the wall originated. He was so engrossed looking at the soaked walls, he failed to recognize the swish of wings behind him.

"You are brave to enter our home alone and unarmed."

The farmer jumped, emitting a high-pitched scream.

"It even speaks as we do."

The apparition facing Liam was so pale, the man couldn't be certain he was not facing a ghost. I—I...

"What is it you desire most, human?"

The fear clouding the farmer's mind evaporated as the face of the chieftain's daughter crowded out all other thought. "Aileen."

The apparition lifted a wing as it crossed its arms. "We hunger for the same beauty.'

Liam shuddered. I suspect you would be the victor of any duel between us.

The creature shrugged. "Yes, but I don't wish her in this form."
It extended a slender hand drawing the gaze of the farmer to the interior of the cave. What he'd presumed to be mist moved with intent and intelligence. Fear gripped his heart.

"Do not fear them. Their hunger is sated."

Liam chose not to believe the creature completely.

"I offer a solution that will benefit us both."

Liam's hackles rose. "I will listen."

"I propose to put the mark of my kind on her, but you must

accompany me. You will be the first being she sets eyes upon, and her heart will belong to you. When your time upon this earth is nearing the end, you must send her to me. I will finish making her one of us to be my mate for all eternity."

Luna paused. The story always drew overwhelming grief upon her soul. She sipped from water Enda placed near her at some point. "What the apparition failed to let the farmer know was all his offspring would carry the mark, and thirst, of the vampire. The name given his flock was a Romanian derivative of the name—Laughlin. As you are aware, Enda, Mc means 'son of'. It's not been but a couple generations since they migrated from the Carpathian Mountains."

"Orla may be beyond your ability to help."

Enda pulled in a deep breath. Luna presented a gloomy picture. However, if he didn't attempt to rescue his sister, he wouldn't be able to live with himself. "Maybe so, but I must try."

"You best prepare your journey soon. I sense he is about to take his clan to a new land. Once he leaves these shores, your chances diminish greatly."

"How may I repay you?"

"Find Orla before too much time passes."

"Of course." Enda offered a bow of respect and exited the cottage, a blessing following him.

"May the Goddess guide you."

Muttering beneath his breath, Enda tromped to his home. "May the Goddess stay out of my way."

His next step would be to employ the one ally he'd garnered in the village of Clan McLaughlin. His hope was the lass would unknowingly reveal the destination of their move. He drafted a note hoping first, the lass would be able to read, and second, she would care to reply. Then, in the manner known and used by many, he put out a piece of bark containing a tasty bit of cheese to call the mouse messenger.

Time tested and true, a mouse appeared at his door. "You wished to send a message?"

Enda rolled his reply into the cylinder to fit in the waterproof carrier on the creature's back. "Please take this to the Clan McLaughlin's village. Find Moira the Red. No one else is to open this but she. Wait for a reply. I'll double your fee."

Before the last word left Enda's mouth, the mouse sprinted toward the southern mountains. Now he needed to gather his supplies for the journey. He looked around the small cabin he shared, had shared, with Orla. The only item he required from this domicile was Orla, and his weapons. Since his sister's whereabouts had yet to be confirmed, he would carry her in his memory. His weapons would fit well in their respective sheaths on his person. His most dreaded task lay ahead — waiting.

Enda paced. He sharpened his blade; practiced mock fighting and, yet, time still moved at its own speed. He stood in the yard, sweat gleaming from his body as he lunged and parried his sword. A quick turn on the balls of his foot followed by a lunge produced a squeal of terror and the frozen form of a mouse messenger, scroll quivering in the holder.

"Apologies, sir." Enda dipped his head in acknowledgement, and withdrew his sword from his imaginary opponent, sliding the weapon into the sheath upon his leather belt. The creature shook until Enda withdrew the note. "Please wait."

He entered his home, locating the largest chunk of cheese he could find and returned to the messenger. "Do you have a method to carry this?"

"There is a pouch beneath my cylinder where you may place it. Thank you, kind sir."

Enda placed the payment in the pouch and executed a quick bow to the messenger. Once the creature scurried from sight, Enda dared to open the note.

Enda, the leader speaks of a new land across the ocean. Some of our clan have settled in a place near the mountains. They send word it is similar to the land of our fore bearers. We leave in a fortnight.

A knot the size of his fist settled in Enda's stomach. Reports from several of his wandering brethren indicated the land across the sea was as vast as the ocean itself. Where was he to look for his sister? He was certain she would not be allowed to communicate outside the captor's kin. Any messages would be monitored. What could he do? He was prepared to trek the breadth and width of the Emerald Isles to find his sibling. But a new land larger than an ocean?

Enda sat on the stone wall surrounding his cottage. The idea started as a tickle in the back of his skull and worked forward. He weighed the pros and cons and, in the outcome, love for his sister, Orla, won over any other consideration.

Enda would rescue his sister by offering to take her place and indenture himself to the McLaughlin Clan.

~ * ~

His plan backfired. Enda groaned as he slid the whetstone over his blade. He lifted his gaze from the blade to stare morosely at the children tethered together being led to the cells. He'd tried sneaking into the McLaughin's camp in the homeland only to be discovered and imprisoned. In a ceremony practiced under the darkness of a moonless night, Enda and his sister, Orla, were bitten and bonded to the clan. Their lives no longer revolved around the sunlight but were trapped to the shadows of the night.

The crack of a whip and scurrying of multiple sets of feet pierced by high-pitched squeals interrupted his reverie. Unbidden tears coursed down his cheek. A quick swipe with the back of his hand removed the telltale traces but could not mend his heart. He would give his existence to free his sister and the wee ones.

Chapter Eight

Cascade Mountains

Killian cocked his head to gaze at the upper rock formation. There were ghosts of images flitting just out of vision. The — impression—was of two tiny beings. In his heart, he could sense the little ones were those he sought. But where had they gone? With the passing of the sun overhead, he calculated his progress would be hampered by the loss of daylight.

He would push forward to investigate the possibility of a pathway leading upward. Watching his footfalls and doing his best to avoid crashing to his death down the mountain, he emitted a blood - curdling scream when he slammed into a leather -clad creature wielding a sword and leading a mount. The other party hollered with as much surprise and volume as Killian. However, it was faster at the defense and had the tip of the sword at his throat before he could twitch a muscle.

"Stop. Lest you wish to lose your head, you will stand still."

Killian eyed the steel blade currently hovering at his throat. The highly sharpened edges reflected light into his eyes. As a master swordsman himself, he recognized the result of hours of careful whet stoning. Should he hiccup, he would lose his ability to swallow. He raised his hands away from his body and weapons.

"I mean no harm."

The being spoke. "It is my desire to pass by you. I do not wish to fear for my safety, so you will hand me your weapons until Pony and I have made it around you."

The fearsome frown on her face discouraged any foolish retort from him. He contemplated the tip of her blade and the warrior wielding it. Undoing the clasp of his scabbard, Killian lowered his blade; his eyes never breaking contact with the she-warrior.

She wiggled her blade his direction. "All of them."

He leaned forward, pulling a knife from the shaft of his leather boots. He placed it next to his sword on the ground.

"Pony?"

"Yes?"

Killian noted the tired response from the animal.

"Pass between us and if he flinches...stomp him."

The animal's ears flattened. "I'll do no such thing. I will, however, crush him against the cliff face."

Killian and the she-warrior stared at Pony then each other, slowly raising their eyebrows. He pressed against the wall of the mountain. "Please pass unfettered. If it pleases, may I have the name of the warrior who's bested me?"

Pony had tromped forward and was snuffling a wildflower attempting to bloom. She lifted her head and watched with interest to see what her mistress would do.

"Why? So you can swear out a bounty on me? I think not."

Killian dipped his head in acquiescence. "As you wish."

The she-warrior sidled away from him. Picking up her pace, Killian watched her trot down the path of the mountain. "Whew! Little demon." He gathered his weapons and when he'd replaced his blades and scabbard to their rightful places, took one more glance toward the clifftop. He closed his eyes and attuned his hearing, but was disappointed to hear not but the sounds of nature. Hairs on the back of his neck prickled as he experienced the sensation of being watched, but the sun was moving to the horizon, and his desire was *not* be stranded in these mountains during the darkness. Tonight was the beginning of the half-moon; a time when the incidents surrounding the disappearance of the young ones would peak.

Killian shivered, a physical effort to shake off the 'watched' feeling, and turned east to estimate the time it would take to place him on the desert plateau. He might be able to thwart an incursion into his settlement if, and this was a big if, the raiding party chose this route. Maybe the knowledge he was poking around these parts would provide enough deterrence for this evening. His gaze swept the surrounding landscape. Normal animal movement was oddly absent. He couldn't sense any life nearby. Busy observing his surroundings, Killian pulled up short before he tumbled into the campground of the spunky swordswoman and her steed. *Idiot. I should have smelled the campfire.*

He observed the pair interacting, clapping his hand over his mouth to smother the snickers trying to escape. It appeared the swordswoman could control him at the point of her blade, but not her horse.

"Pony, please. We have one, maybe two more days, and we'll be there. We're more than half the way."

"I'm tired, and I don't want to GO anywhere but home. My hooves hurt. I think my shoes are too small. My back hurts, my stomach hurts and every muscle in my body is sore. I want to go home. NOW!"

She dropped her head to her hands and moaned. "Goddess, protect me from the stubbornness of intelligent animals. Pony, you promised to complete this trek, all of it, after which I'll retire you."

Pony snorted. "That promise was made before I had all the facts."

Her groan carried to Killian's hiding place. He bit his lip to stop from laughing.

"If this were easy, there would be no need for bribery, would there?" The she-warrior's measured tones spoke to her waning patience.

"Fine, but I expect the best hay available three times a week."

"What? That's blackmail."

"Agree to it, or I'm leaving for home immediately."

For several minutes, a heavy silence permeated the air.

"Fine," she grumped. "See you in the morning."

"Humph." Pony turned her back on the swordswoman, swishing her tail to flick at imaginary flies.

~ * ~

Killian curtailed his progress until the she-warrior and her companion were far enough away the morning shadows had lessened. He insured his presence would not be noted by returning the area where he camped to the pristine state in which he found it. The trek down the mountain felt easier than trekking up. Maybe it was his hurry to arrive at his living quarters before the rising of the half moon. He really had no desire to be in the open when the night creatures started to roam the woods.

Pebbles skittering across his path halted his movement. His instinctive reaction was to peer up, the rising of the hair on his arms giving him the sensation of being tracked. His gaze met with two glowing red eyes belonging to a gnomepire. *In this new land?*

"Enda?" the name automatically sprang to his lips. "What— how?"

"No time. Return here on the morrow when the moon rises high above the mountains. I'll try to gather as many of the kidlings as I can and meet you at this spot."

Before Killian could reply, the face of a former warrior and compatriot disappeared into the surrounding tree line. He continued his journey, contemplating the encounter. The warrior Enda had been one of the bravest he knew, but his sudden disappearance surprised everyone. The rumor had risen he'd been attacked and slain.

Killian found the truth to be stranger than the rumors. Enda was alive and aware of the plight of the children. His ruminations had occupied his mind for quite a while as the land before him flattened to the high desert he'd grown to love. Though the terrain evened out, Killian was unable to spy the warrior and her Pony. Maybe she'd chosen to ride and make up for lost time. It would've been nice to attempt a conversation without the blade of a sword at his throat. He could hope for a rematch after he'd rescued the children.

By the intensity of the sun, it must be reaching mid-day. He could be at his abode before nightfall. He idly wondered where the she-warrior was.

~ * ~

Recognizable changes in the horizon alerted Tiamoon to the presence of a community. "I don't think we have too far to travel now, Pony. I can see what appears to be a settlement."

Pony whoofed out a breath. "I sure hope so. My back and legs and hooves…"

"I get the picture. The best grain in the valley and never doing this again."

"Nice to know you were listening."

"I heard that."

"I meant you to."

"Alright my amazing steed and friend. May we canter the last mile or so? The sooner we arrive, the sooner your tribulations will end."

"Fine."

Tia smiled as Pony slowly worked into a canter, quickly settling into a comfortable rhythm. Less than ten minutes later, the pair were entering the outskirts of a community. Tia surmised the inhabitants must be gnomekind because of the distinctive architecture of the homes. The family's goddess preference was obvious by the direction of the front door of each building. Slowing Pony to a walk, Tiamoon admired the care put into the maintenance of the yards and upkeep of each of the homes. It proved her mother wasn't the only fussy gnome around. She'd been particularly interested in one home when the front door opened and the occupant stepped into the daylight.

"Tia? Is that you, little Tiamoon?"

"Not so little anymore," gruffed Pony.

"Shhh." Tia steered Pony toward the front gate of the house and stopped. She realized she was looking at a replica of her mother, but with opposite features. Where Skye, her mother, was fair and light, this woman was swarthy and dark.

"Tiamoon?"

"Yes." She dismounted Pony and tethered her to the fence.

"No, no." The woman unwrapped the reins and led Pony to the rear of the home and a barn. With a deftness belying her stocky form, she had Pony free of her saddle, reins and all other items. A bucket of clear water sat in a specially built container and fresh, sweet hay lay in a feeding box. As she closed the stall door, she commented. "I hope that will suffice."

Pony muttered something, but it was unintelligible past her full mouth.

Tia chuckled. "It will suffice."

The woman looked at the she-warrior. "I would not be able to pick you out in a crowd, but..." she picked up a wayward strand of red hair. "...your mother's hair was close to this shade when she was a child. She'd deny it now, but I was there and can testify otherwise."

"Then I can assume you to be my Aunt Luna?"

"I am."

Tia was noting the immaculate state of the interior of the stable. "Do you ever house animals here?"

"Of course."

"The interior is cleaner than most homes I know."

Luna chuckled. "I have a very fussy stable hand who becomes quite trollish if every piece of straw is not in the right place."

"Are you sure he won't mind Pony being here? She can be quite...messy when she wants."

Pony lifted her head from the feeding trough and laid back her ears. "Hey..."

Tia shot her a piercing look. "You know it's true."

The small horse shifted her head away from the warrior. "If you say so."

Luna bit her lip to suppress a laugh. "He will tolerate it and not complain. After all, he works for me."

Pony sniffed and moved to the water pail effectively dismissing the two-legged individuals.

Tiamoon and her aunt secured the stall door. They meandered through the barn and into the courtyard between the home and barn. Luna forged on to the house while Tiamoon slowed her pace. The air was different on this side of the mountains. It was lack of smell that triggered Tia's reaction. She couldn't smell green. No aroma of ripening field grasses; no tickling of tree buds against her nose; no familiar floral scents reminding her it was spring. Everything just reeked of...dirt. That was the key element. All she smelled was the sand on the ground and dust particles drifting through the air. Moving to the house, a familiar pungency assaulted her.

"Ugh. Melons. If I never see another one, it will be too soon." She knocked lightly on the back door and entered when invited. "Is there a place I may store my belongings until we leave?"

Luna escorted her to a small tastefully furnished room containing a chifforobe. "I do believe this will serve the purpose. When you've unloaded your bags, please join me at the dining table. I've made tea and berry scones to go along with it."

"Thank you. I'll be there shortly." Tia placed the saddlebags on the floor and gingerly sat on the single bed. The top was cushioned, but below the first two inches, the base felt firm. She knew her sleep this night would be blissful. She peered through the window, admiring the deep blue of the sky overhead. In her valley, the sky was blue—between rain showers. She could get used to the dryness but would miss the greenery. Tia sighed, "Always a choice to make."

The small cottage made traveling from room to room a quick affair. In the dining portion of the kitchen, Luna poured another cup of tea and slid the plate of scones toward her niece. "I would venture to guess you might be as hungry as your four-legged friend."

The aroma of freshly baked treats set Tia's mouth to watering. "You'd be right. I could eat a bale of hay myself." Filling her plate, she stopped trying to decide where to start. *At the beginning, silly.* Picking up a particularly plump scone, she felt the warmth permeate her fingertips. The explosion of rich, sweet flavor in her mouth was a slice of heaven. She moaned in ecstasy.

"Now *this* is worth fighting for."

Luna's deep chortle reminded Tia of her location and set her cheeks to burning in embarrassment.

"I think I'll take that as a compliment. Eat as much as you like. I can always make more. It will be nice to have someone to appreciate my cooking."

If all her meals are this sumptuous, my waistline is going to suffer.

Tia watched Luna putter in the kitchen, aware of how much like her mother the woman moved. When the dark-haired female sat across from the warrior, Tia began to compare the two sisters, noting how they were almost exact opposites of one another. Skye, as her name indicated, was a vision of lightness, save her steel colored eyes. Luna reminded her of the night sharing the same odd colored eyes.

"You're wearing an odd expression on your face, young one. What troubles you?"

Tia dropped her gaze to the plate before her. "No trouble, Miss Luna."

"It would please me greatly if you would call me Auntie. You are, after all, the child of my younger sister."

"Of course, Miss Lu...Auntie." Familiarity with any but the beasts made Tia uncomfortable, however, she was here at her aunt's request. "I do have a question."

"Ask."

"Why did you request my presence here? I'm sure you have myriad warriors whose talents far outweigh my own."

Luna nodded. "Aye, that we do, but our warriors have approached this problem from near every angle we can fathom, and we find we are no nearer a solution than the day it began."

Tia allowed silence to settle over the table. After a few moments where the only movement was that of the dust motes dancing in the air, she continued. "I'm afraid, Auntie, I don't know what your problem is. Therefore, lending my expertise would be—fruitless."

Luna blinked her steely blue eyes then emitted a giggle. "How silly of me. Everyone in our community is consumed with this issue. I just made the mistake of thinking you would just—know.

"Let us resolve this conundrum immediately. Our young ones have been disappearing in alarming numbers at every half-moon. We have launched massive searches with the entire village scouring the surrounding areas for days and peering into every crevasse on these plains. We've had no success in locating the children. When we finally give up and go home, some of the lost turn up at their doorsteps, but they are..."

Tia watched Luna search for words.

"...not the same. They are listless and appear lifeless. They can't remember where they'd been or what occurred."

"Has anyone thought to question them?"

Luna's expression of horror indicated to Tia that avenue hadn't been explored.

"Why would they? The children say they can't remember."

Tia realized she needed to tread very lightly. "Most children are aware we adults don't wish to frighten them or cause bad memories. However, straightforward, honest answers are most likely to come from a child.

"Might there be an older child who would agree to speak with me?"

Luna stood and crossed to the front window. She paced back and forth in front of the glass, muttering and shaking her head. After several minutes, Tia's aunt turned to face her.

"I believe young Jacob would be the best candidate. He is a bit older and was one of the first to go missing. Each time the half-moon rises, his mother says he locks his bedroom door and doesn't emerge until the moon is full or wanes. He tried to tell his family about his experience, but his parents allowed their disbelief and doubt to show through. They were unable to get him to speak of it again. "

"Maybe a stranger, willing to listen," Luna directed an intense look Tia's direction, "without making judgment might have better luck. "

Tia moved toward her aunt and placed a hand on her arm. "I will try my best to appear as open as I can. It's time we found a starting point to this problem."

Luna nodded. "Not a minute too soon. I'll send a message via the bird network. I've fresh bread in the oven. You can take a loaf with you. We need to end this horror before another child is taken. "

Chapter Nine

Cascade Mountains

Orla sat against the stonewall adjusting to keep from crushing her wings. There were some advantages to her new situation she liked. The wings came in handy. She looked to her left at the figure reclining on the floor. Leaning forward, her wings rustling slightly, Orla tucked a wayward strand of light brown hair behind his ears. This little one refused to leave her side. When the overseers tried to take him to the young masters, he screamed, bit and created such a violent scene, they soon backed off.

No hostage was worth the physical punishment this tiny villager doled out. What they didn't know was Orla instructed the youngling to behave accordingly. The herders counted on their charges being terrified of them and submitting without question. They were unprepared for a fighter.

She began to hum a lullaby her mother used to sing, the melody stirring happy memories.

Beneath the towering oak tree,
There lives a little gnome.
He wanders far and near
But always comes rambling home.
For home is where he is happiest,
His needs are always met,
Home is where the sun shines,
Home is the best.

Orla smiled at the mental picture she cherished of her mother;

46

arms wrapped around her daughter, rocking in the big oak chair in the little girl's room. The routine continued until Orla was nine or ten at which time her mother gently reminded her she was nearly grown and quite large for her mother's lap.

A chuckle escaped her lips and the youngling near her moved in his sleep. *I really wish I could find a way to release these children. They shouldn't have to pay for the sins of their parents—or me.*

Light into her crevasse dimmed, and she slid close the inner lid to hood her eyes, another new feature, to find the source of the shadow.

"Enda? Why have you come, brother?"

The shadow quickly morphed into the nearly unrecognizable form of her sibling. He, too, sported a set of wings and his eyes glowed an eerie red in the lower light of the evening.

"I was worried about you. Orla, you've ceased attending the nightly meals. Why?"

Orla rose from the floor and stretched the wings. "I find my appetite sorely diminished with the thought of eating food in its uncooked state."

"I agree but starvation is not the best option. Besides, I find that due to our—inconvenient—transformation, I'm developing a taste for blood. At present, small forest creatures fill my need. Should I ever start hungering for more, well, dear sister, I'll have to determine a permanent solution to this purgatory."

Orla's wings wavered with her sigh. "Yes, I, too, have experienced the same thought. My present form grates against all the teachings we received as children." She dropped her gaze to the form at her feet. "They are so young to endure such horror."

Enda could naught but agree. "We need a champion to help fight for us."

"True, but there are so few left in this new world."

The siblings shivered as the round up call was trumpeted in the distance.

Enda turned. "I need to be there to make sure our charges suffer the least amount of harassment. I believe McLaughlin has some fear of me."

Orla emitted a small chuckle as her brother exited the cave. "If you knew how much Sean fears you, you'd realize just how powerful your position here could be, but I can't tell you or he has sworn he will murder each of the children individually and force me to watch."

She grew pensive and paced the cavern floor. "I must find a way to let Enda know his true worth here. It's a knowledge that will give him enough power to turn this situation around. But how?" She ruminated over her predicament until an interruption from one of the taskmasters. He barged into the cave, startling Orla.

"What do you want?" She glared at the hefty brute.

"The child is ordered to the meal table by the master."

"He will not leave this shelter."

The overseer puffed up his chest and moved toward the sleeping child.

"STOP!"

The shout halted the beast in his tracks. "You will not touch this youngling."

"But..."

Enda held up a hand. "This will be on my shoulders. Go tell the master you did your best but met resistance."

The overseer spun on his heel and trotted to the center of the village.

Orla gaped at her brother. "You will bring the wrath of Sean upon us. Not only that, you've endangered all the children."

Enda cast his gaze upon the sleeping child. "No. I've a plan I hope will give the children their freedom-forever."

Orla raised an eyebrow. "We're talking about what's-mine-is-mine-and-what's-yours-is-mine Sean, right?"

Enda allowed a smile to grace his face, a rare sight these days, Orla noted.

"I have faith my offer will be acceptable to him. Let's join the others."

"This young one will stay. I fear for him. These sessions weaken him and, at this rate, he will expire soon."

Enda noticed this child hadn't seemed as resilient as others, and Orla voiced the concern he felt. "I agree. If the others have issues with it, they may go through me." He offered his hand to his sister, and they trudged to the area where the meals were served.

The din was deafening and Enda sent a worried look Orla's direction. "It sounds as if they have begun the games."

A crease marred her perfect forehead. "I'm afraid so."

The pair entered the area and were distressed to view the village children scampering for a place to hide while the gnomepire children hunted them. One gnomepire child held a village youngling on the ground. His teeth were lengthening as the downed youngster screamed in fear.

Just as the gnomepire prepared to sink his teeth into the neck of the other child, Sean opened his mouth and emitted a screech that halted all activity. "You may have a small taste, but do not drink your fill. Until we bring up new guests, we must conserve our stock."

Orla felt her stomach roil. She would readily welcome death versus this daily hell. Enda needed to figure out a plan and quickly. She had a strong will power, but the pull of the blood thirst was eroding her resolve.

Sean called the gnomepire children to the head table, rewarding each for their prowess. The taskmasters rounded up the village captives marching them back to their cells. Platters of raw meat and vegetables were brought to each child along with a tankard of water. Few of the younglings had the strength to do more than drink the liquid.

When one of the taskmasters reported this to Sean, he roared. "Force them to eat! It will not do for any of them to expire."

The overseers hunkered down and centered their attentions on the pale prisoners. They raised their whips and drew back their arms. A blur of beating wings accompanied by the flash of a sword stopped them.

"You will stop there or risk skewering." Enda's eyes blazed a deep ruby.

The overseers shrank from the warrior-pire wielding a sword. One slipped from the cowering group to race to the dinner area and inform the master.

"A sword? Where did he acquire a sword?" Sean's eyes bulged in anger, and he rose from his place at the head table, knocking over his chair. Spreading his wings, he darted to the prison cells. As spoken by his overseer, Enda stood brandishing a sword at the intimidated taskmasters.

Sean screamed his disapproval. He glared at Enda. "DO NOT CHALLENGE ME in my own community!"

Enda stood firm. "I will do whatever is necessary to protect these children."

The master fluttered to the ground, advancing on Enda, his overseers moving as a solid wall behind him.

"I do not fear death. In fact, dying would be welcomed if it released me from this curse. But before we advance to that point...I have a proposition to offer for your consideration."

Sean abruptly stopped, causing several of the overseers to bump into his back. He pivoted and graced the group with a steely glare. The large creatures shrunk back a few steps and affixed their attention on the dirt beneath their feet. Once he'd controlled the immediate situation, Sean returned his attention to Enda.

"A proposition? What makes you think I want to hear any sort of proposition from you?"

Enda worked to hide the smirk trying to break out on his face. He dared to look the master directly in the eyes. "Because you have nothing to lose by listening and everything to gain." He watched Sean mull over his statement.

"Speak."

"You consider yourself a great warrior..."

"I *am* a great warrior," Sean's wings snapped open.

Enda noted the tips shaking. "If you are such a great warrior, by rights, your offspring will be great warriors, too."

The master lowered his wings and folded them against his back. "Yes. They have my hunting instincts and determination."

"So why do you soften them by bringing village children for them to hunt? Why not require them to hunt small animals such as rabbits?" He watched the anger bubbling to the forefront of the master's emotions.

"They are still young."

"Yes, but your ancestors didn't hunt children, did they? The elders made them wait until the younglings were grown and exhibited a cunning borne of experience."

Sean worked this bit of information around. "I suppose this has something to do with the village children?" It was his turn to smirk.

"I am certain you know the answer—yes."

"Tell me the rest."

"I propose you release all the village children."

"No."

"I will swear complete fealty to you and do anything you ask of me."

The stubborn glare on Sean's face softened as he considered the possibilities. "Anything?"

"Anything."

"What of Orla? Do you speak for her?"

"I can't speak for my sister. The decision must be of her own volition."

The overseers, distanced and silent to this point, grumbled. The tallest of the group spoke. "You can't allow this, Master. Who will provide the blood source for the pirelings? Who will gather the wood for the fires and the mushrooms for the table, Master?"

Sean spun on the ball of his foot to face them. "Silence! Do not presume to tell me what to do."

The group leader stepped back into the formation.

"In fact, go to the dining area and clean up."

Astonishment washed over their faces immediately followed by grim looks hiding anger. "Yes, Master."

Sean turned his attention to Enda. A sneer had replaced the smirk, transforming his ruggedly handsome features into a hawkish mask. "I will consider this after the rising of the half moon. Once the moon begins to wane, I'll give you twenty-four hours. If," he grimaced a smile, "you are able to gather all the flatland children and remove them from the mountains by the end of said time, I'll hold you to your word and require you to swear your complete loyalty to me and my house until your death."

He made a show of standing at attention, setting his face in a serious expression and placing his hand over his heart. "I will give my solemn oath not to seek or harm any of the children."

Enda felt his heart flutter with a small ray of hope. But he knew Sean well enough to know he might be agreeing to this for the moment, but he was holding something back. "Thank you."

Sean executed a small bow from the waist and spread his wings, flying to the dining area.

Enda was left watching over the exhausted youngsters. Most were deep in sleep, barely able to make it to their assigned cells. One young man struggled to stand.

"Stop. I'll come to you." Enda stepped around little bodies arriving near the youngster and took a seated position. "What is so important you would resist the urge to sleep?"

The boy leaned against the rock wall of his cell. "My name is Patrick. I used to live in the village in the flats below."

Enda was aware of these facts, but it appeared important to the child to relate them. He waited in silence.

"My cell mate is Maeve. A couple days ago when we were out hunting mushrooms and collecting firewood, we heard, then saw, one of the men from our village who is touted to be a fearless warrior. I pushed some pebbles over the cliff's edge, and I believe I attracted his attention.

He peered up and searched the cliff top. Before we could say anything or send down more signal rocks, the overseers cracked their whips over our heads.

"I've felt the whip, but Maeve is too young, so I guard her against the possibility. She is not doing well and weakening with each day. I heard you with the Master. I can tell he is certain you won't succeed in saving us, and I think he might be right. I'm one of the strongest here, and I would have a tough time trekking down the mountainside.

"If you are to make it to the valley floor, the first settlement is ours. The two homes nearest this mountain belong to the shaman and the warrior, Killian. They might be willing to help you remove us if asked." Patrick turned his young face to Enda, tears gathering in his eyes. "I really want to go home. I miss my family." Patrick lay down and drifted to sleep.

Enda paced while running over the simple, but possible, plan put forth by the youngster. Leaning down to touch his shoulder, Enda spoke when the boy's eyes opened. "You have offered a plan I believe can work. I must wait until the sun sets before I attempt to leave. Tell no one except my sister, Orla. Do NOT allow her to follow me. Should there be questions about my absence tomorrow, tell them you heard me mutter about finding the perfect hunting ground for the pirelings and saying it might take a day or two."

"I'll return as swiftly as I'm able."

Patrick acknowledged Enda's request.

~ * ~

Enda made the rounds of the holding cells visually checking the children and taking a head count. Most were showing the wear of their ordeal. Some of the smaller ones concerned him. He hoped young Patrick was right about the warrior Killian. Enda had lived long enough to accept the fate he'd chosen but the little ones still had lives to live, mates to find, and the chance to produce their own offspring.

He stood at the opening of the prison cave, the need to move nagging him. Pulling deeply of the clean air, he watched the sun disappear below the horizon. He spread his wings and leapt into the sky. Sean would not miss him until the morn. If young Patrick did his job convincingly, Enda had approximately forty-eight hours to complete his mission. He rose above the treetops by mere inches, making his escape. He should arrive on the valley floor within a couple hours.

He flew through unfamiliar territory, not having been included in the village raids. Desperation he would never see the last of the forest ended when the craggy ridges smoothed to rounded hilltops and sparse sage plants. As predicted by young Patrick, a smattering of tiny white lights dotted the valley floor not far from the foothills. He began tipping the lower part of his wings in to slow his descent and soon touched the sandy desert. The sky above opened to reveal thousands of stars sparkling against an indigo background as far as his vision allowed. Not even in his homeland had Enda witnessed such a sight.

Light glowed warmly from the windows of the first abode nearest him. The second abode was darkened. "No one home, I guess." He broke into a run seeking a place to shelter him until he worked up the courage to approach the cottage. Behind the small home stood an outbuilding where he sensed another being resided. Dashing from his temporary cover to the large door, he maneuvered the open space with little to stop him and quietly slid open the entry. He turned to peer at the abode and consider his next move.

"Who are you?"

The voice startled him causing him to whirl about and throw open his wings. Widening his pupils, he noted a pony in the furthest stall. He tip-toed to the enclosure.

"Did you say something?" Enda stood speaking to the only other occupant of the building...a small horse.

Pony snorted. "Yes. I said, who are you?"

The gnomepire closed his wings and tucked them to his body. "My name is Enda. I'm here to locate a warrior named Killian. I was told he lives nearby. Do you know of him?"

Pony narrowed her eyes as she looked over this strange being. "There was a man we encountered on the trail to our destination. He carried the weapons of a warrior. Maybe the shaman knows him. "

"Shaman?"

"Yes. That is her cottage, and this is her barn."

Enda recalled the conversation with young Patrick. There was mention of a shaman close by. He quickly worked the situation around in his head. Having a shaman see him first might just be a bonus. While she may not have seen this type of gnome, she would be aware of their existence and less likely to overreact. *It's now or never.* He nodded Pony's direction. "Thank you for your help."

Pony was nodding in sleep, the affairs of two-legged creatures being none of her concern.

Enda strode to the barn door and shut it once he was outside. He decided to take a chance and walked to the back porch where he knocked and waited. There didn't seem to be any movement inside, but he wanted to be sure before moving elsewhere. As he raised his fist to knock again, the door opened.

Chapter Ten

High Desert, Central Oregon

Tia held the bread in her hands, the warmth shimmering through the towel wrapping. She scanned the area as she moved to the house a quarter mile away, noting landmarks to be held in memory. She was feeling naked without her sword and dagger, but agreed with Luna that an adversarial approach worked—sometimes, but this was not such a situation. As directed by her aunt, there was a little flaxen-haired girl playing with a tiny dog and a young man occupying a wicker chair on the front porch.

"Hello there. I bring greetings and a gift of food from Luna. May I approach the house?"

The little girl scurried to the porch, dog clutched tightly in her arms, and hid behind the young man.

"Who asks?"

Tia noted his extreme wariness. "I am Tiamoon, daughter of Skye and niece of Luna. I bring fresh bread for the family and a desire to speak to Master Jacob."

"Mom! There is someone here to see you." The young man held his arm around the little girl moving them toward the front door.

The top had been opened. Now the bottom portion of the Dutch door swung open. A solid young woman with light brown hair put a hand above her eyes to shield them from the sun. "Are you Tiamoon?"

"Yes, ma'am. I am."

"I've been expecting you. Your aunt sent a bird message earlier this afternoon. Please enter the yard and come inside the house.

Maryann, Jacob? Inside. The sun will soon be setting, and it is the first night of the half moon." She had no sooner gotten the word *half* out of her mouth and the two youngsters scurried past her into the house interior.

Tia sensed the overwhelming fear permeating from the two younglings. She entered the cottage finding it a bit larger than her aunt's but laid out in a similar fashion. Heading to the kitchen area, she placed the bread on the counter then watched the backs of the children as they disappeared down a narrow hallway into doors on opposite sides of the house. The snick of latches confirmed the two were tucked inside their rooms.

The young woman extended a hand toward Tia. "I'm Terra. I'm sorry for the abruptness of my children, but Jacob has recently returned from a very bad experience."

Tia clasped the extended hand. "I'm Tia. I'm sure Aunt Luna gave you a bit of explanation as to why I'm here. First, of course, is to deliver her bread baked just this morning but, also, I thought I might speak with Jacob—alone—and see if he might be able to help me in my task."

Miriam allowed a sad smile to touch her lips. Her golden eyes pooled with the beginning of tears. "I'm so sorry, but I think your trip is for naught. Jacob won't speak to anyone about his time...away."

Tia felt the need to push the issue. "May I try?"

Terra straightened, her accommodating mood dissipating into a protective mode. "I'll ask him if he will speak with you. However, if he says no, you'll not pursue this further."

Tia nodded her agreement. "Of course." She watched the woman stop at the first door in the hall. After knocking, she entered for several minutes, finally emerging with the young man following her.

"I'm not sure why, but he has agreed to speak briefly with you. May I suggest you speak on the porch? That way when you have completed your questioning, you may feel free to leave."

Tia recognized a dismissal when she saw one, but her opportunity to speak to one of the youngsters who'd been abducted was too important to be bothered getting upset about his protective mother.

"Thank you. Jacob?" Tia indicated they should move out front.

The young man led the way, taking up the wicker chair he'd been sitting in earlier. Tia hunkered down so she was lower than the child and waited for him to speak first.

"What do you want? I tried talking to my parents, but they didn't believe me. The village people avoid me as if I were covered in boils and spitting venom. Why should I believe you are any different?"

Tia kicked her feet from beneath her and sat on the wooden boards of the porch. The move was to buy her time to formulate and answer for Jacob. "I don't know you. Therefore, I have no reason to believe, or not believe, you. All I can do is offer an ear for you to tell your story with no judgments. I need information to help the other children still...out there." She watched as the young man worked over her answer.

He peered into her green eyes. "You'll listen without making any faces or asking any questions until I finish?"

"I will."

Jacob weighed her answer against his knowledge of adults. He obviously felt she was telling him the truth, but he would've thought the same of his parents. They punished him for lying and making up tales to scare his sister.

Jacob began, his voice quiet and measured. "It was one day before the half moon."

Tia watched the young man shiver from head to toe.

"I'd just hunted down Maryann. She had taken off to find her dog, Pepper. We knew of the disappearances but weren't scared because our dad was working in the woods with other village fathers gathering timber for house building. We felt because he was nearby, we were safe.

"Anyway, Maryann's dog chased a rabbit to the edge of the hills, and she went after him. When I found the two, they were sitting under a tree resting. I gathered them up, and we started walking back home. The sky began to darken, and we picked up our pace, moving faster to get home sooner. We saw the lights of the village come into view, and Maryann broke into a run. She was carrying her dog. I could tell she was frightened. I didn't run because, well, I'm older and a boy. I'm not supposed to be afraid.

"I'd reached the lane in front of our home when I was suddenly in the sky, the earth dropping far below me. A faint scream reached my ears, but I didn't know who it was. I found out later it was Maryann. She watched as the creatures snatched me from the road."

Jacob stopped for a moment and closed his eyes. He lay his head against the back of the chair and took several deep breaths. "I was juggled up and down like I had been on a real horse when I rode. My stomach was beginning to feel funny, and I thought I might throw up. About that time, I noticed I was being brought close to the ground. I figured I could jump up and run away but I was wrong.

"The creature flying me had very sharp, strong claws and held me tight while someone else put a bag over my head and tied my hands. We took off again and flew higher. I could tell because the air got colder, and I was shivering. After what seemed like an hour, I felt my stomach starting to roll again and knew we must be coming down from the sky. I was put on the ground then made to stand up and pulled to a cavern. Once inside, I was shoved on the ground and told not to move. I really wanted to take off the bag, but they threatened me if I did."

Jacob watched Tia as he spoke. She didn't move from her spot and, true to her word, didn't interrupt. He continued his story, happy to tell someone who might believe him.

"I was jerked up from the ground and pushed forward for about five minutes. I fell a couple times but was told to keep moving. I could hear other feet shuffling so knew I wasn't alone. Once we got to the destination, my hood was ripped off my head. I faced a long table set for a meal, but there was no food on it. The creatures sitting in the chairs looked like me, but they had red eyes and wings. They talked funny, too. The guards were bigger, almost the size of humans, and ugly. They turned us around. There were four boys, including me, and four girls. I recognized several of them from the village. Patrick was one of the first ones to be taken.

"Someone at the table screamed out, and we were pushed forward and told to run and hide. I didn't know where to go but chose what I thought was a good place behind a big rock. Within a couple minutes, a kid near my age, but looking like the creatures, yelled that he found me. He grabbed my hands, still tied together, and dragged me back to the table. All the others had been found too.

"When we were all returned, the guy sitting in the middle of the table nodded his head and..."

Jacob stopped. He swallowed and pulled deeply of the air. "...the kids' teeth begin to get long in the front. They grabbed our arms and bit into the wrist then started sucking. I'm not sure what happened next, because I passed out. When I woke up, I felt sick and started throwing up. I'd been put in a cell with Patrick, and he was trying to help me feel better."

Tia noted the color in Jacob's face drained and he was ashen. "We can stop if you like."

He cleared his throat and continued. "Thank you but I want to finish this and forget it."

Tia nodded.

"Patrick was being held to keep the new prisoners from getting too scared. He protected many of us from the overseers, that was what the big guys were called, and made sure we had enough food. He's also the reason I'm here and not still up there."

Tia lifted a brow. "Oh?"

"Yes. What we were being used for was to give the young pirelings, as they called themselves, practice on how to capture and feed on wild game. We were the game they tracked at dinner. I didn't do very well at getting better after they took my blood so Patrick talked with the big boss. He told him if they drained all our blood, the villagers would hunt them down and kill all of them to the last one. He said I was too sick and needed to be released.

"When he came back to the cave cell, he told me to stop eating and try to look as sick as I could. It wasn't hard to do because I was feeling as bad as he'd told them. After a week, they picked me up, flew me back and released me in front of the house. The following month another kid was snatched."

Tia sat and watched as the young man slumped against the back of the chair. The telling of his tale had drained him and reignited fears. "Thank you, Jacob. This has been difficult for you, and I appreciate you sharing your story with me. May I ask a question or two?"

Jacob turned wary eyes to her. "Maybe."

"Could you guess where you might have been taken?"

When Tiamoon didn't question his story, Jacob was obviously relieved. It had been a weight lifted from his shoulders. But her question made him think. Could he guess where he was? "I believe we were in the mountains because I could smell green, you know, like trees and stuff. There were deer hides in the caves on the floors and, somewhere close by was a stream. I could hear it at night. But that's about all I can remember."

Tia waited a moment before asking, "You say it took you about an hour, flying, to get to the encampment?"

"Yes."

Tia mulled over the youngster's story. His parents and the village folk might consider him a liar, but Tia's aunt and mother were shamen and verified the gnomepires Jacob spoke about existed. Apparently, they, along with many other refugees, moved from the old country to America.

"Jacob, you are a very brave young man. I know your story is true. Thank you for sharing with me. Your experience will help me to locate the others and bring them home."

Jacob wiped unbidden tears from his cheeks. "Thank you for believing me. Now I know I'm not crazy."

Tia shook her head. "No. Not crazy and lucky to be alive. I'll bid you good night."

As she departed the cottage, she heard the front door being closed and the snick of a lock. The half-moon was near its zenith. All the villagers were taking precautions to stay safe.

I best do the same thing and get to Luna's with all haste. Tia picked up her pace and broke into a run. *I really need to get out and do more of this running stuff.* She was a master at up-close-and-inside situations. Her knife had seen many a battle as well as her long blade. Those scenarios didn't involve running any amount of distance. Why should they? She always remained upright as the victor. Her ruminations served to pass the time until she darted through her aunt's cottage door, slamming and leaning against the heavy wooden enclosure. There was no bolt to slide or she would have ensured it was latched as well.

Must slow my breathing. She knew if her breathing slowed, so would her heart giving her a better chance to ruminate over what young Jacob imparted to her. By thinking rationally, she would have an opportunity to devise a workable plan. Thudding in her ears indicated she was not being successful in her attempt. She leaned her head against the wooden plank and closed her eyes tightly, picturing the small stream trickling past her mother's home. The vision was working. The pounding in her ears seemed to be subsiding allowing the sounds from within Luna's home to tickle her consciousness. She noted the usual creaking of wooden beams cooling for the evening and...breathing from two sources.

The fragrant aroma of fresh baked bread still lingered, but beneath the hunger-producing smell she detected something—else. Something masculine. Tia peeked open her eyes to view the face of the stranger from the mountains wearing an amused smirk on his face.

"You!"

"Me, what?"

"What are you doing here?"

"I was invited. And you?"

Tiamoon crossed her arms. "I was invited, too."

As the stranger opened his mouth to reply, Luna bustled into the room on her way to the kitchen area and set the kettle to boil. She turned toward the living room area and noted the two occupants.

"Oh, I see you've met."

Tia scowled. "Yes and no. This...being was trying to impede my path on my journey here."

The smirk left his face, and he spoke. "I was not. I was searching."

Tiamoon puffed out a breath. "More likely looking to rob honest travelers."

Before the stranger could take up the verbal challenge, Luna held up her hand. "Stop right this minute. You are both here at my request, and for a specific purpose; the *same* specific purpose. Tia, come in to the living room and sit down. I'll ready tea."

The she-warrior stomped around a chair nearest the door and plopped down, crossing her arms and scowling to make certain he was aware of her state of mind.

Luna pulled two tea bulbs from her silverware drawer and filled them with her own blend of calming leaves. She placed the bulbs inside her teapot and gathered the dishes to share the beverage with the youngsters. Putting everything on a serving tray, she turned and moved to the living room area and placed the tray on a small serving table. The silence within the small cottage hung heavy in the air.

She raised up and put her hands in her apron. "You are both adults, yet, you act as young as the missing. Tiamoon, this," she waved a hand in the stranger's direction, "is Killian?"

"Vineyard."

"Vineyard. Master Killian, this," again, she turned Tia's direction and waved her hand, "is my niece, Tiamoon of the Glen."

Both parties gave barely perceptible nods.

Luna poured tea into the cups and stepped back allowing her guests to doctor their cups. She remembered she had scones in the kitchen she wanted to serve and moved to the cupboard.

"Well, Tiamoon, if you and your pony had not stood in my way, I would probably have completed my quest. But you were in such a hurry..."

"Please. You were standing with your mouth open gaping at the wall of rock looking for all the world like an owl caught in the daylight—"

"STOP!" Luna placed the plate of scones on the serving tray and held both hands toward the opposite sides of the room.

Tiamoon and Killian sat on the front edge of their respective seats, mouths open, fingers pointing at the other in a frozen state. Their eyes were blinking furiously.

"I was so hoping the two of you could get along without any—assistance—but I see I was mistaken. Because of your contrary natures, this conversation will be one-sided until I have had my say." She moved to Tiamoon where she gently closed her mouth, lowered her pointing finger to the arm of the chair and settled her against the back. She moved to Killian and performed the same routine.

"The children of the valley have been disappearing for the last six months. Some have been returned in various states of shock and terror while others are still missing. Both of you are hardened warriors whose skills are languishing in peacetime. It is up to you to find out what is happening to our young ones and solve the mystery then bring them home. Together. As a team. Do I make myself clear?"

She waved her hands in the air as if wiping away a spider's web.

Tiamoon and Killian's bodies relaxed into the chairs. They glared at each other and straightened their clothing.

Luna scowled at the pair. "Well?"

"Yes, ma'am." Tia mumbled.

"Of course, Miss Luna." Killian stared at his hands placed on the arms of the chair.

"Tia, you made a visit to young Jacob. Did he share any information with you?"

Tia opened her mouth to answer when there was a knock at the back door.

Luna's brow furrowed. "Who could that be at this hour?" She walked to the door and opened it mere inches to peer at the nighttime visitor. "Goddess. Come in."

Tia and Killian exchanged apprehensive looks.

A creature resembling a gnome with wings followed Luna into the living room. Its eyes were red and glowing slightly, wings trembling.

Luna placed a gentling hand on the creature's shoulder. "This is Enda."

Tia narrowed her eyes to view the creature more clearly. Indeed. This was the same creature who'd dropped by her camp on her journey to Luna's. "Wow. What happened, Enda? You were once a gallant warrior. How did you come to..." she waved her hand up and down, "this?"

Enda sighed, the action causing his wings to shudder. "I tried to rescue Orla only to fall victim to her curse. I would've left, but I don't wish to leave her to fend for herself. That was my original reason. When the clan moved to this place and started stealing your young, I knew it would be up to me to protect them until a solution was presented."

"Enda, may I offer you food?" Luna started toward the kitchen.

"No. My appetite has changed, unfortunately. Thank you for your kindness." He turned to the pair sitting in the living area. "Are either one of you Killian?"

The sandy-haired young man nodded. "I am."

The creature blew out a sigh. "Wonderful. A young man named Patrick sent me to find you and explain the situation."

Killian smiled. "Wonderful. Your news of him eases my mind. How is young Patrick?"

"He has made it his mission to watch over the youngsters as much as he can. He works closely with my sister, Orla, in protecting them from the cruelty of the overseers."

Killian knew what this man-creature said was probably the truth. The Patrick he knew was always monitoring the younger children and protecting them against bullies. "What is happening to our children? Why do they return acting so oddly?"

Enda pulled a small stool from against the wall to his location and took the opportunity to sit for a moment. "While in the old country, life continued in the village of the McLaughlin as it had for generations. The children born chased after small creatures of the woods to learn how to satisfy their blood lust."

Killian started. "Blood lust? What are you talking about?"

Enda pulled at his wing, removing a burr from the leathery surface. "The clan McLaughlin is born of an old curse from the Carpathian Mountains. At the turn of the century, a writer from our home of Ireland penned a novel about the McLaughlin clan. It was titled, Dracula."

Killian sucked in a deep draught of air. "Vampires? There's no such thing as vampires."

Enda looked at the warrior. "I only wish that were true. I'm sure you noted my wings; they're hard to miss, and the color of my eyes have changed to this hideous shade, so I may see more clearly at night. When I can't control the blood fever, my teeth inch their way out of my mouth so I may use them to feed the fever.

"This is the reason I'm here. When the clan relocated to America, they knew little of the wildlife in the mountains. Their pirelings were dying because they didn't know the scent of the local animals for hunting. One of the overseers noted to Sean, the clan's master, a village nearby with children. He suggested a raid be made, and a few children brought to the camp in the mountains and used as...bait."

"What?" Luna dropped her cup, the fine china shattering on the floor.

Tia spoke. "This verifies what Jacob told me."

Enda turned his gaze to her. "Jacob is well? That is good news. Orla will be pleased. At our evening meal, I swore an oath to the Master. I told him I would give him my complete loyalty if he allowed me to return all the children to their homes."

The room was silent as all those gathered listened.

"He agreed to the arrangement after the half-moon wans and only for forty-eight hours. If I don't have them returned to their homes by that time, they will stay at the camp until the master deems them no longer useful. I need your help to ensure they arrive home safely.

"The second part of my deal included the caveat he would not steal children ever again, and I would provide the small animals he felt necessary to teach the pirelings how to become gnomepires."

Enda started to pace. "If I could just find a way to lay a trail for you to follow, like breadcrumbs mentioned in the children's tales, I could be certain the younglings would arrive home safely." He stopped his endless trek, standing to ponder a solution.

Luna initiated a search through her kitchen drawers. "There used to be a cloth covered..."

Tia focused her attention on her aunt when the woman mentioned *cloth covered*. "Of course." She sprang from her chair and trotted to the guest room. Once inside she directed her search to the saddlebags she'd brought. She dug through each until she located the package she sought. Quick stepping into the living room, she stopped in front of her aunt.

"Mother said to give this to you."

Luna opened the offered bag and retrieved a piece of stone the size of her palm, holding it to her heart. The unusual stone was a blue green in color and flat as a dinner plate. Near the upper right corner, a round hole the size of a quarter existed. "This could be the answer. I'll be right back."

She headed to the back of the cottage where she slept, closing the door behind her. Midway down a set of drawers in the dresser, she opened the middle one and pulled out a similar bag. With a practiced hand, she undid the knot and opened the top to upend the bag. A quarter-sized white stone with blue hue fell to the top of the dresser. "Moonstone," she whispered the name in reverence.

Placing the turquoise on top of the dresser, she worked the stone into the hole, twisting slightly to secure the pair together. The moment the connection was correct, a low vibration filled the room. Luna stared into the mirror above the dresser. Within moments of the vibrations, the face of her sister appeared in the mirror. "Skye. You look wonderful."

"As do you, Luna. What is it you need of me?"

"I'm afraid there is need of our combined powers to thwart an evil from the old country. An evil brought from the mainland of Europe long ago. How soon can you arrive here?"

Skye left the mirror frame returning with a knapsack in hand. "I can be there before the setting of the half-moon."

Luna released a pent-up breath. "Excellent. I will see you at that time. Travel safely, sister."

"I will, thank you."

Luna placed her hand on the mirror. Skye followed her lead. "We need to imbue the stone with a bit of our essence. I intend to use it for an emergency. Will you agree?"

"Yes."

Together the pair chanted.

"In dark of night

Or bright of day,

Let sparkling lights

Lead the way."

The stone on the dresser sparkled iridescently shooting one star to touch each shaman, slowly dimming once the task was completed.

Luna placed the amulet in the canvas bag. "I believe we shall meet with success. I await your arrival, sister."

The image in the mirror faded. Luna picked up the talisman and returned to the living area.

"Wow. You've given your word you'll be his devoted follower if he allows you to free the children?" Killian's expression conveyed disbelief.

Enda was looking anxious until Luna entered the room. "Mistress."

She gentled his anxiety with a simple touch on the forearm. "I believe I can offer a solution."

Three gazes centered on the shaman.

Luna explained. "The bag brought from the west side of the mountains has a partner on this side. Inside, a portion of an amulet rests. Apart, they are strong. Together, they hold great power which may be bestowed upon the carrier." She drew out the form for the warriors to see. The two stones formed a scene of blue green sky and white moon. Luna placed the amulet within the bag and turned to the former warrior, Enda. "Take the stone from the bag and hold it in your hands. Will you be able to fly?"

He nodded his affirmation.

"Keep repeating, 'moon and sky' with each wingbeat. You'll be leaving a trail we can follow, day or night."

He stared at the small canvas holder in his hand. "Will I be able to see the trail?"

Luna patted his arm. "No. It will be visible to those searching and no one else."

"Thank you. I'd like to stay and rest, but there will be trouble if I'm gone too long." Enda nodded at the others in the room and exited out the back door, Luna following. She stopped him before he leapt from the ground.

"Do you wish to remain in this form?"

He frowned. "That's an odd question."

"Well, do you?"

"No. I'd wished to pair and have younglings as most do, but I've seen many years on this land. The younglings are just beginning. It is their time, not mine."

Luna smiled and stepped back. "Remember, moon and sky, moon and sky."

"Farewell, Mistress Luna. Moon and sky, moon and sky."

Luna witnessed the shower of sparkles falling from between the gnomepire's hands. She was sure he was unaware of the trail he was leaving. She knew to Skye and her, the signs would be visible up to a week. The younglings would be home in time for the summer equinox.

Chapter Eleven

Cascade Mountains

Enda felt foolish, but chanting the 'moon and sky' mantra seemed to make his wings stronger and powered him through the air at unbelievable speed. Whatever it took to get him back to the encampment before Sean suspected. He spotted a valley so close to the clan's home, it surprised him. Surely there were small animals available for the pirelings to hunt. Then the truth of the matter hit him. Sean didn't want the young pires to taste animal. He wanted them addicted to the taste of human blood. The fury rising in Enda's blood pushed him to fly even faster. As his feet touched the ground, he opened his mouth and bellowed in anger. The air vibrated with the heat of his rage.

The sun was creeping over the hills. Morning was breaking in the McLaughlin community. The overseers sat numbly inside their barracks awaiting orders for the day. The women were scurrying around putting together what semblance of breakfast they could and the pirelings were stumbling about rubbing the sleep from their eyes. The air undulated with a noise so intense all the members within the area clasped their hands over their ears.

Sean burst from his abode, sword at the ready. "What the hell was that?"

The women shrunk in terror. When the master was angry, everyone suffered. Orla stepped up to the head of the clan. "I believe my brother has returned. From the sounds of it, he's made an unfortunate discovery." She narrowed her eyes and directed her gaze straight at him. "I think he may have come to the same conclusion I have. You have no intention of allowing him to take the children home, do you?"

A sneer appeared on Sean's face. "Now, what would make you think I would go back on my word?"

Orla huffed a breath. "Because your word is worthless. You have no honor. You *promised* my brother you would free me if he became part of the clan; let me see, what was the wording? Oh yeah, 'for a short time.' It has been near two decades since you kidnapped me, Sean McLaughlin. You are a black hearted creature with no soul." She turned and wended her way back to the cave to care for her young charge.

Sean screamed at Orla's disappearing back. "Come back here! You can't talk to me like that. I *own* you." He stomped to the table in the clearing slamming his blade on the top. "Bring me something to eat. NOW!"

Orla entered the cave and checked on the youngling. He was not doing well and would expire if not seen by a shaman. She was shaking from head to toe. *Can't believe I spoke to him like that.* She surprised herself. Maybe she was as strong as Enda thought. As if summoned, her brother entered her cave.

"Orla. I believe I have found a way to get the children back to their homes safely." He moved to a smooth-topped boulder and sat. His wings were sagging and all his back muscles ached. Clutching the stone in his hands, he dropped his head and blew out a breath.

"What's this?" Orla slid the amulet from Enda's hands. The flat stone was a beautiful blue containing a white stone in the upper corner.

Rather unconsciously, Enda mumbled. "Moon and sky."

Orla looked at the stone. "Yes. I can see it. What does it mean?"

"Rescue."

She lifted a brow and turned to ask him what he was talking about only to face a prone figure snoring on the ground. Enda had slipped off the stone and fallen asleep. "He must be exhausted. I'll ask when he wakes."

She listened to the commotion outside as she slipped the stone into Enda's hand. The rest of the village was preparing for the half-moon ceremonies tonight. The moon would be at its zenith and strongest for the pirelings purposes. She worried for her young charges. If help didn't arrive soon...no, she couldn't think the worst. It was her chosen responsibility to keep them healthy. Given the poor food Sean fed them, it was a miracle any of the youngsters could still give the pirelings a workout. She smiled. *The tenacity of children amazes me. Were it that we all had the same drive.*

~ * ~

Luna felt the presence of her sister before she saw her. A quiet knock on the door announced the arrival of the other shaman. "Come in, sister. Your trip was very quick."

Skye placed her backpack on the ground and hugged Luna. "I sensed an urgent need."

"There is. Our village children have been disappearing for some time now, and we were at our wits end as to the reason. Some would reappear but have odd behaviors. All who came back were terrified of the half-moon."

Skye's forehead wrinkled in thought. "Gnomepires?"

Luna's mouth dropped. "Why is it you thought of this immediately, and I couldn't fathom such a happening?"

Skye chuckled. "Because, dear sister, my side of this land has more troubles than you can imagine. If it could happen, it has. The only curse we haven't suffered is—gnomepires."

Luna smiled. "Ah well, at least you're prepared for the event. I believe our two warriors need a purpose, and this seems appropriate for them. They seem to have started off bumping heads. I hope they can work together to save the village children."

"Tiamoon will step up when the time comes. She loves having the world think her prickly and hard to get along with, but the truth is she is very caring. Don't tell her I said so. She'd never forgive me."

"Let me show you where you'll stay. I'm going to bed down in the barn."

Skye spoke up. "Sister, don't do this for me. I've spent my share of nights on the ground trying to sleep before a big battle. I'm used to it."

Luna smirked. "You forget, so did I. I find the openness of the barn allows my brain to work better. Now, let's get you settled. I know the half-moon will be tonight, so I think if we arrive just before the ceremony, we can take care of the problem and have the children home before the rising of the sun."

Skye settled her backpack on the bed in Luna's room. "I agree. Their power will be strong but, together, we are stronger than they can imagine. Good night, Luna. I'll see you in the morn."

~ * ~

Tiamoon heard the mumble of voices as she flipped, yet again, on the bed. The mattress was softer than her own, and the goose feather pillow made her nose itch. Sitting up, she threw back the covers. "I can't sleep. Maybe a walk in the fresh air will help." She pulled on her britches and boots, topping off with her leather smock. A duster would protect against spring's bite and provide cover for the sword she now strapped to her side. Tip-toeing to the door, she opened it with as much stealth as she could. The hall was clear and the mumbling she heard must have been in her head, because it appeared the house was locked down for the night.

When she'd asked Luna about a key, the shaman laughed. "No need. Most of the valley residents are a bit afraid of me. I'm not about to let them know I don't stir up a bubbling cauldron of snails and lizards. Let them wonder."

Tia slipped out the front door and past the gate; the half-moon providing enough light for her to feel comfortable without a lantern. She took the road toward the mountains. Finding a spot to sit and contemplate, Tiamoon started, emitting a squeak when a voice interrupted her thoughts.

"Can't sleep either?"

She jumped up, bringing her sword to the ready.

"Whoa! You are too inclined to hack and slash with that thing." Killian moved into the light from behind a tree. "I'll leave you to your thoughts. I was walking and, when I saw you head this direction, figured you wouldn't want to be anywhere near me. I got the message earlier. I'll be on my way."

Tia sheathed her sword. "No. I'm just jumpy. I was angry earlier, because I have a suspicion my mother and aunt have a hand in trying to pair us. I'm not ready for a pairing. Sorry."

Killian laughed. "Don't feel alone. I think you're right. Luna has been on me about settling with one of the village girls. They're all very nice but putting my swords in storage for a horse and sheep or worse, a plow, is not my idea of living. I'm not ready to be paired either."

Tia smiled. "Stay and talk with me. I'm confused about this whole situation. How could one of the best warriors I've fought alongside become...this, this thing?"

"It does seem outlandish, doesn't it? I would not have thought such a thing possible until I asked Ms. Luna about it. She gave me a brief explanation of how such evil could exist in our world. It's here now, and I will do all in my power to rescue the children, even if it means my own demise."

Tia cast a glance Killian's direction. His fair hair caught the moonlight, giving him the look of a halo about his head, his jaw set with determination. She sensed the seriousness of his statement. "I will offer what expertise you may need. These little ones don't deserve the horror Enda spoke of to us. I can't even imagine their terror."

Killian sighed. "Nor can I. I've been searching the mountain for the last two months since the snow melt, but experienced little in the way of success. I hope Luna has a plan that will help end this agony for all of us."

The pair sat in silence for a moment. Killian was the first to speak. "We should head home. We'll need to be sharp in the morning. Are you ready to go back?"

"I guess. I really was hoping for a battle where I could use my sword, but those days are over."

"I'm afraid so. It begs the question, what do old warriors do when there is no war?"

"I don't know. Shall we?" She'd stood up.

Killian moved to her side, and the pair walked back to the cottages. The morrow would bring new challenges neither could imagine.

Chapter Twelve

Gnome Village, High Desert

Skye placed her extra britches and shirt in the top drawer of the dresser. Her mind whirled with impressions and solutions. If they were to avoid physical violence, they needed the element of surprise. The only way she could see them surprising the gnomepires was to arrive when least expected; the middle of the night or dawn when all the celebrating was taking its toll on the pires.

She sat on the bed and pulled on her boots. *No time like the present.* Grabbing the walking stick she'd set in the corner, she headed to the back door. As she reached to grab the handle, the knob twisted and opened. Luna stood before her.

"We must leave now."

Skye nodded agreement. "My thoughts precisely. I'll fetch Tiamoon, and we can bring Pony in case some of the little ones are unable to make their own way."

Luna turned. "I'll saddle Pony. Meet me in front of the cottage."

Skye started toward the room where her daughter was sleeping when she heard the rattle of the front door. She stopped and watched Tiamoon come in. "It seems none of us can find time for rest this night. Your aunt and I have determined to give ourselves the advantage of surprise; we need to leave—now."

Tiamoon's glum expression immediately changed to a rarely seen grin. "I'll get my hauberk and knife. One can't be too prepared." She bolted to the guest room and gathered the needed items returning to join her mother. "Let's go."

The pair exited the cottage making sure the door was securely closed. They spotted Luna leading Pony to the road. Tia was surprised to see Killian standing and waiting.

He smiled and gave a quick salute. "I see everyone has the same idea. Let's hurry. I wish to have this particular quest done and over as soon as possible."

The party agreed and started up the road to the mountains. Skye held her staff in front of her and, before too long, sparkles appeared on the ground.

Tia came up next to her mother. "What are those?"

Luna smiled. "Bread crumbs."

Tia dropped back next to Killian, and they exchanged confused glances. "What made you decide to come back to the house?"

Killian blew out a breath. "I realized I've gotten soft in my village lifestyle. Were I in a true battle, fatigue, weather, and numerous other inconveniences would be of no consequence. A warrior battles until the war is won or he loses his life. If we are to avoid bloodshed, for the children's sake, then we must use the element of surprise. Waiting until the sun rises gives the enemy more opportunity to duck and hide, or stock up for an attack, imagined or real. We need to get into the encampment, find the children and escape with little or no conflict. That meant leaving right away."

Tia was silent as she walked next to him. "How ironic we all think alike. My aunt and mother had the same idea."

Killian allowed a smile to escape. "Your aunt would surprise many if they knew of her past."

Tia stared at him. "How do you know?"

"There was an elder gent when we first settled in the valley revered as a great warrior and who, rumor had it, ruled a mighty clan in the old country. He often spoke of the battles he fought. Luna not only healed warriors, but she doled out her fair share of wounds to many enemies. I guess she was quite the sight in her battle armor. Old Risteard's eyes would sparkle when he mentioned her."

"I never knew."

"Few do."

The company continued to follow the sparkles and were at the mountain village before much time passed.

Killian turned to Tia. "How did we arrive so soon? When I was searching, it would take the better part of three hours to reach the trail to the top."

"Did you not hear Skye and Luna mumbling?"

He nodded his head affirmatively. "I just thought they were...well, I don't know what I thought."

"They were uttering spells. I guess they slowed time or speeded up our progress. In either case, we truly have the element of surprise."

Killian looked at the few buildings located beyond a tree line up against a rise of rocks. "Indeed."

Skye noted. "The trail of dust ends at those caves. I'm guessing the young ones are held there.

Luna looked around. "I agree. We are too exposed in this location. Let us find the nearest cave, and maybe those inside can direct us to Enda. We should leave Pony here. There is no need for her to suffer."

"Thank you. Bad enough you woke me." Pony grumbled.

Tia and Luna grinned at each other.

The four gnomes tread lightly to the first opening they saw and entered. Inside the cave, a fair-haired gnomepire sat cradling a child and humming a lullaby. Luna approached.

"Orla?"

The gnomepire looked up. "Who is asking?"

"It's Luna."

The humming stopped followed by a quiet sob. "I didn't think anyone would ever come."

Luna knelt and placed her hand on the shoulder of the weeping gnomepire. "We've been searching since the moment we got the message you'd been taken. We never gave up hope."

The child began to stir and mewl quietly. "Little Alvin is not very strong. I fear for him."

The conversation stilled as the sound of two sets of heavy footfalls headed their direction. A lantern light glowed near the opening of the cave.

"Where can we hide?" Tia whispered.

"You may try to hide behind the rocks at the back of the cave, but if someone comes in, there is no shelter from discovery."

The four scurried to the few mid-sized boulders up against the back wall. Crouching as low as they were able, they huddled together and listened.

"What is going on?" The voice was rough with a guttural hint. "I heard voices. Who's here?"

Orla looked to the overseers. "No one. You heard the little one fussing."

"No. I heard voices." They entered the cave and immediately headed to the back. "HA! Get up. Come on, move." The largest beast prodded the four fugitives from their hiding spot. "Well, well. Who do we have here? The shaman, Luna, and Killian. Not a very good warrior, are you?" He snickered at his pun, looking to the other overseer. "Move. The master will be very pleased to see you. March."

Tia looked to her mother and raised her eyebrows in question. Skye just smiled and followed the first beast. Shaking her head, all Tia could do was trail behind. When the group reached the center of the village, the lead taskmaster held up his hand.

"Stay here." He looked to his partner. "If any of them looks to escape, bash them." The second grimaced a smile and smacked his spiked weapon against the ground.

"With pleasure."

Luna and Skye appeared unusually calm for the dire situation. Tia seethed, aching to draw her sword and thrash the beast, but wasn't sure what the consequences to the children would be. *I hate not having the upper hand.* She glanced Killian's way and noted his reaction similar to her own. He appeared vexed at having been captured so easily and quickly.

The beast pounded on the door of the largest abode in the village. All the homes were snugged against the rocks and built to blend with the surrounding forest lands. Once again, the beast pounded upon the door, and jumped when it swung open.

"What is it you want?" A rumpled Sean McLaughlin glared at the creature, his eyes burning red with irritation.

"Uhm, uh, Master? We have some unbidden guests." The overseer extended his arm, his weapon clutched in the hand, to indicate the group in the center of the village.

"Well, do something with them. Why was it necessary to wake me in the middle of the night?" Sean growled.

"Sean McLaughlin. You are a coward and a murderer." Luna stepped forward.

"WHAT?" The clan leader bolted from his home, snapping open his wings, and flew to face his accuser. "I should have known. Luna. What are you doing in my village, old woman? No one sent for you."

Luna stepped to within a foot of him. She looked him in the eye as she spoke. "Ah but they did. Every child you have stolen and abused or killed with your blood lust has called to me. It's time for you to pay back the debt."

The master burst into laughter. "Right. You're going to make me *pay back* those who gave willingly to my children." He turned to the overseers. "Waken the village and bring them here. I want them to see what happens to those who think they have power over me. This will be a lesson for *all* to learn. Guard them. If they move, kill them."

Luna stood her ground as the gnomepire winged back to his home. He entered and closed the door. She turned to Skye. "It has begun."

Skye dipped her head in agreement. She started moving her lips.

Tia turned to Killian. "I don't know exactly what is happening, but be prepared for anything. My mother and her sister are up to something."

Luna joined Skye, and the pair stood placidly, lips moving.

It took the overseers twenty minutes to gather the villagers and prisoners to the town center. The dinner tables had been placed so the residents could sit and watch the happenings. When all were gathered and seated, the head overseer strode to the master's abode and knocked.

The door swung open and Sean stepped on to the porch in full regalia. He wore a cape tied at the neck. There were slits to allow for his wings. He'd changed into black trousers and a formal white shirt. The cape bore his family crest on one side, and he sported a sword at his waist. He stepped forward, and the villagers clapped politely.

Most were half asleep and not sure why they were needed in the town square. Sean descended his steps. He strode up to the two sisters and spoke for all to hear. "This will be my finest hour. Not only will I show my power, but I'll rid myself of a plague brought from the old country." He turned to the overseer nearest him. "This plague can only have been brought here by Enda. Bring him here to share their fate."

One of the beasts located Enda and shoved him into the two sisters. In the shuffle, he missed the exchange of the amulet from beneath Enda's wings to Luna's hand.

"Now..." Sean strut around the captives, a wicked smile covering his face.

"Wait." Luna voiced.

Sean stopped. "What is it you want, old woman?"

"If you are going to terminate my existence, then I would like to say something."

A look of irritation crossed the master's face. "Fine. Have your say, but don't be too long-winded. I have much to do for tonight's celebration."

Luna slanted a look to Skye. "How many here have been changed willingly?"

The villagers shared looks. A few hands shot into the air.

"The rest of you are captives in a sense, yes?"

The question brought some hushed conversation among those present.

Sean stepped forward. "What are you doing? What does it matter how my people arrived here? Let's get on with this. No more questions." He moved to speak directly to the villagers. "No one shall doubt my authority. If I choose to use the children of the gnome village, or even those of the Others to train my pirelings, it is my right as the Chieftain of this clan. Those who question or doubt will receive punishment or death." He turned and nodded to the overseers.

Luna and Skye continued their muttering, only now, they were being vocal and raising their voices with each cycle of the spell they wove. Luna held the turquoise portion of the amulet, and Skye the moonstone.

The evil of this curse
Has torn lives apart,
Return those who wish
To the beings of their heart.

Tia noticed the voice of the clan leader seemed to disappear, and all she could see was his lips moving and his hands gesturing. Then the sparkles began. In a cloud reminiscent of desert dust devils, a small circular tornado of sparkling particles appeared in the center of the square. It grew to encompass everything in sight, blinding all. For several minutes, there was naught but sparkles to be seen. Then the cloud slowed and the sparkles disappeared. When the wind ceased, silence descended on the gathered gnomes.

A buzz erupted. Soon there was excited chatter and laughing. Someone broke into an old Celtic tune and several danced in the center of the square.

Skye and Luna shared a hug. "Old women, my foot!" Luna complained.

Tia and Killian looked around to witness no gnomepires - anywhere. Tia was awed. "What happened?"

Skye moved to her daughter's side and put her arm around the warrior. "I am a shaman just like your aunt. But the whole truth is we have magical powers we chose not to use very often. Your aunt's question let us know most of the village people here were captives of the curse of the McLaughlin's."

Tia looked around. "Speaking of which...where is the master McLaughlin and his overseers?"

Luna chuckled. "See those pink-eyed possums? That's the overseers. And the bat fluttering in the trees is Sean. They morphed to the beasts most like them. They are masters of all they rule now." Luna looked around and winked at Skye. "The only thing missing is snow."

The pair faced each other and recited. Soon there were snowflakes falling from the sky. The children were giggling and screaming in delight.

Tia shot her mother an exasperated look. "Why snow? It's cold and my boots will get wet, and..."

Skye laughed. "Because it feels like Christmas. Let's gather our children and go home. Tia, bring Pony so we may put little Alvin on her."

The others agreed and found the village children close by, Patrick standing guard around his friends. Tia brought Pony who complained loudly, but ceased her whining when she saw how ill the young man was. With all the children gathered, Skye and Luna instructed everyone to hold hands. Little Alvin held Enda's hand on one side, and Orla's on the other. The sisters smiled and a sparkling cloud enveloped the group.

Epilogue

High Desert

Pony complained about her hooves hurting and her back and...the list was endless, but Tia knew she was thrilled to be going back to the green of the valley.

"I hope you don't mind, Auntie, but I think I want to see what this side of the mountains holds for me."

Luna smirked at her sister, Skye. "Not at all, child. You're welcomed to stay as long as you like. I'll enjoy the company."

Tia headed to the front door whistling.

Luna slid her arm around her sister. "I hope you won't mind a fair-haired warrior for a son-in-law."

"Luna, don't push. I suspect they will probably end up together, but in their own time. Meanwhile, I really need to get back to my garden. Now that I don't have a rogue warrior tearing it apart every time she gets bored, I might be able to keep some food in my house."

Luna hugged Skye. "Be safe, sister."

"You, too."

~ * ~

Tia knocked on the door and waited. It opened and Killian motioned her inside. "Thank you. What's going on? Your note sounded urgent."

Killian pulled out a chair from the table for her. "I have something I wish to discuss with you. With Luna's potion helping the children to heal and forget their ordeal, my job as village watchman has ended. I received a mouse message from a schoolmate who emigrated to someplace called Japan. Seems there is a war brewing there, and he asked if I'd like to come help. Our kind is being used to serve as spies for America. Are you interested?"

Tia's green eyes glowed. "Am I? When do we leave?"

The End

www.ingramcontent.com/pod-product-compliance
Lightning Source LLC
Chambersburg PA
CBHW070642130626
46555CB00006B/2672